# *Greenwillow*

# Greenwillow

## by B. J. Chute

GREEN MANSION PRESS

NEW YORK

# Greenwillow

By B. J. Chute

GREEN MANSION PRESS
NEW YORK

© 1956 by B. J. Chute
© renewed 1984 by B. J. Chute
Reprinted by permission of Elizabeth Hauser
Published by Green Mansion Press LLC
New York, New York  10021
Visit us at www.greenmansionpress.com

Publisher's Cataloging-in-Publication Data
Chute, B[eatrice] J[oy]  (1913 – 1987)
Greenwillow/ by B. J. Chute.
p.  cm.
Summary:  In the rural village of Greenwillow a young man
falls in love but is convinced that he is doomed to wander and
can never marry.
ISBN 0-9714612-3-6                    LCCN 2002111350
[1. Country life — Fiction. 2. Marriage — Fiction.
3. Faith — Belief and Doubt — Fiction.]
[Fic] – dc21        2002                    P-CIP

Interior illustration by Melanie Hall

Printed in the United States of America

*For*
*MY MOTHER*

*Greenwillow*

# CHAPTER ONE

LONG AGO, centuries perhaps, the village of Greenwillow had been stood in the corner and forgotten.

A river ran through it, a river that came down fresh and fast from the tall hills, and, once away from the village, grew very important and tossed up debris along its banks: mills and flat-roofed factories and towns called Cheever and Middlemas and Croke. Beyond Greenwillow, this river was called by another name which no one in the village troubled to remember, but here it was the Meander, having let itself grow tame in a swamp that was all goldcups in the spring and bordered with dark-berried catbrier at the autumn turn of leaves and sun.

Bedded down in wide soft marshland, it paddled about for a bit, giving great pleasure to the blackbirds and water thrushes, and then it slipped docilely between green banks and entered the village. By the time it passed the steepled and sober church, with its two pastors and its two front doors and its two ways of walking before the Lord, the Meander was as narrow as a needle and as polite as a pussycat.

On this September Friday, with the sun clear and just high

enough in the sky so the chickweed had opened all its wandering blossoms, the Reverend Birdsong was moving with sedate haste along the Meander's south bank and addressing the river nicely in Latin.

"*Ave, fluvius,*" said Birdsong, a bit hazy about the vocative but showing a very cordial spirit.

The Reverend Lapp, matching his fellow-churchman's gait, frowned. He found Latin displeasing, not for its syllables but because he sincerely felt that if the Lord had intended His Word to be circulated in an alien tongue He would have so advised His deputy at Greenwillow. This assumption was not as failing in humility as might be supposed since, on two occasions, the Lord had taken the trouble to instruct Lapp at first hand, once on the matter of the unflagging authenticity of hell-fire, confirming Lapp's own natural bent, and once on the doctrine of Infant Damnation. As revealed truths, however granite, he had no choice but to accede to them, and it was to these angelic trumpetings that Greenwillow owed its plural clergy.

The winter Sunday on which the Reverend Lapp had risen, very tall in the pulpit, and announced the immediacy of hell for the benefit of his congregation was a famous one. The Devil, he said, was walking the countryside and gathering in his own, and since it had been forty-odd years since anyone had indisputably seen the Devil (a Mr. Proudfoot, long gone to his reward) his listeners naturally reacted with a proper sense of gratification. It was clearly recollected that a rafter in the church had groaned; there was a rumor, less well documented, that it had muttered Amen. The congregation had gone home feeling like lily pads, their faces offered to the sun and their roots in most infernal places.

Attendance at church the following Sunday was unusually

large, and a less dedicated pastor might have been satisfied with their roused interest and toasted only their toes in the fires of hell.

Unfortunately, on the preceding Thursday (a bad day, Thursday, falling as it does nowhere in the week at all) the Reverend Lapp had been seized by another vision. On Sunday therefore he was constrained to thunder, with appropriate regret, that all babies who had slipped like little minnows through the nets of baptism would be sent to hell without hope of salvation.

This time, it was not only the church rafters that muttered. Hell, felt Greenwillow, was no place for a baby.

On Monday, a deputation with bonnets and folded hands, headed by Mrs. Aggie Likewise, called on the Reverend Lapp. The intention of the deputation had been to leave the reverend his hell but to take away the babies; however, the theology somehow grew mixed and Aggie got cats into it. Granting that Aggie was partial to cats, it did seem as if they might have been excluded this once, but she dragged them into the conversation by their tails, fretting over the kittens' spiritual survival just as the reverend was quoting Jeremiah. In Old Testament midstream and incensed at the interruption, Lapp broke off to rebuke Aggie and to announce that cats had no souls.

Aggie rose and marched out of the parlor, her upright back a reproach to all, and she would not return although Mrs. Lapp (the minister's mother and something of a cross) had borrowed and was still in possession of Aggie's counterpane pattern, an intricate embroidery with flowers so pleasing that butterflies had been known to come in at the window and frolic on the bed. Mrs. Lapp refused to surrender the pattern and Aggie refused to cross her threshold and snatch it from her, and there the matter rested in an extremely cross-grained manner.

In the meantime Greenwillow was revolving in its mind. The more vigorous members of the congregation had taken rather kindly to the revitalizing effects of hell. It put salt in the sermons and kept the pews from nodding, and they became inclined to regard the softer Christians as mere thistle-puffs. As for the babies, it was maintained that all right-minded Greenwillow babies gathered naturally at the font, and that any infant who rashly chose to be born outside Greenwillow had worse things to contend with than the Devil.

The anti-damnation side continued in attendance because there was nowhere else to worship but, spurred by Aggie Likewise, they took to praying for their minister's salvation and asking forgiveness for his sins. There can be few things more irritating to a man of the cloth than to be continually prayed over, and the Reverend Lapp would go home from church and wrestle with himself at some length, his opinions of Aggie being grievously unchristian.

Here, however, the matter rested uneasily until the strange arrival, the following spring, of the Reverend Birdsong. He presented his portly figure on the doorstep of Greenwillow at eleven o'clock of a bright May morning, carrying in one hand a wicker case and in the other an open umbrella full of white-cupped hawthorn blossoms. He said the Bishop had sent him.

This was most improbable. No one, not even the late Mr. Proudfoot, had ever seen a bishop and to their knowledge no bishop had ever been advised of the existence of Greenwillow. Lapp had come to them unannounced some years ago, exactly one Sunday after his predecessor, the Reverend Cloud, had settled confidently to his final sleep in the green-gray churchyard. Before Cloud there had been a Witchett; and before

Witchett a pastor who was so enamored of the Meander that he had finally drowned in its waters where they hurried beyond the village, and who could still be seen on starlit nights, walking its banks and composing his sermons.

Uncertain as the background of Greenwillow clergy might be, therefore, one thing was clear. When needed, they came; when needed elsewhere, they departed. But never before had they been supplied in twos.

The proper course for Birdsong to have taken was that of backing courteously out of Greenwillow with a murmured apology for carelessness on the part of the Bishop (if one believed in the Bishop). This course he did not take. He spent the afternoon of his arrival sitting on the banks of the Meander; he spent the evening under an elm tree until the dew began to fall, at which point the Reverend Lapp's Christian charity began to prick and, against his mother's well-expressed objections, he offered Birdsong the spare bedroom. This Birdsong accepted happily, bringing the dew in with him and freshening Mrs. Lapp's carpet. He asked for very little except a pitcher of water for the hawthorn, explaining that he could not otherwise fold his umbrella, a logical point.

The following morning, over a breakfast of porridge and milk, Lapp made it quite plain to Birdsong that the village already had its spiritual needs well attended and then set him on the doorstep, pointing out that the path to the next town was clear as the river it followed. Birdsong nodded wisely and departed. Lapp watched him go and returned to the house with a sigh of relief, closing his door on all the jubilance of May.

Mrs. Lapp, watching from behind the parlor curtain, observed him come in, rubbing his hands in self-esteem, and let him rub just long enough to get up a good glow which she might douse. "Left his hawthorn," said Mrs. Lapp. "Not to mention his umbrella. Not to speak of the wicker case."

"Oh, dear," said her son with really formidable restraint. "Oh, dear, dear."

"Talking to Aggie Likewise, he is now," said Mrs. Lapp from her eyrie by the curtain. "Since when was she abroad so early?" She clucked. "Raised his hat to her, he did."

"He took his hat with him?" said the Reverend Lapp with pale hopefulness.

"Took his hat, left his umbrella." She added suddenly, "It's my belief Aggie's not long for this world. It's always the healthy ones that's the first to go."

"We must pray for her soul," said Lapp.

Mrs. Lapp said she would think about it, but her tone was not encouraging. At this moment the Reverend Birdsong detached himself from Aggie Likewise and came trotting back to the Lapps, waving in a friendly manner as he came. Mrs. Lapp, being above peering out of windows at her neighbors, did not wave back. Lapp himself went to open the door.

"A golden morning," said the Reverend Birdsong, shaking sunlight off his shoulders like a puppy coming up from a bath. "I have come to relieve you of my worldly goods."

"You're leaving," said Lapp happily.

"Well, yes and no. Your amiable neighbor, Mrs. Likewise, offered me asylum."

"It's the right place for mad people," said Mrs. Lapp, wilfully misunderstanding.

"A roof over my head," said Birdsong gently. "I used the word loosely."

"I don't believe Aggie did anything of the kind," said Mrs. Lapp. "And I don't believe the Bishop sent you."

Birdsong gazed at her. "What bishop?"

Lapp said coldly, "You told us that the Bishop sent you."

"Did I?" said Birdsong perplexedly. "Ah, so I did." He gave them a sudden pleased smile like a baby who has finally managed to grasp its toes. "And so he did, so he did. A good man."

Lapp frowned. "Do I take it, sir, that you intend to lodge with Mrs. Likewise?"

"Precisely. She has an extra room which the cats are not using. There are fifteen cats, you know, and I may have missed a kitten or two. They were all out in the garden, behaving in a very secretive manner, so one had to count them by their tails. I may have counted a tail twice here and there. Or missed a tail." He nodded affably. "Well, no matter, they are all in God's hands."

A small shiver ran across the parlor furniture as if, aspenlike, it was about to dance up a storm. Mrs. Lapp hugged herself in anticipation. Her son drew a long breath and raised his eyes to a heaven limited by the parlor ceiling. "Cats," he said, "do not have souls."

Birdsong beamed upon him. "So Mrs. Likewise said. Or rather, so she said that you had said. I expect," he added dreamily, "that would be why the Bishop sent me."

He then departed for the spare bedroom and returned with his umbrella and wicker case but without the hawthorn which he had left scattering its untidy, inedible petals on the floor. A bee had come through the window and, what with feeling that it would be reckless to interfere with a bee and the fact that his own waistline was ill adapted to stooping, the Reverend Birdsong left the whole matter for Mrs. Lapp to clean up.

Downstairs, he found that Mrs. Lapp was not speaking to him, confining her opinion to a series of sniffs. Her son accompanied him to the door and they stood together on the stone step while three pansy-faced Likewise kittens watched from the garden border.

"You plan to stay permanently?" said the Reverend Lapp. "In Greenwillow?"

"I shall preach," said the Reverend Birdsong.

"There is only one church here," said Lapp. "It is mine."

"Loaned to you," said Birdsong.

Lapp sighed. He was a fair-minded man and there was much truth in the observation. "What is your position on hell?" he said heavily.

Birdsong answered with some diffidence, "We have it on very high authority that gladness of the heart is the life of man."

"You consider hell problematical?"

"Irretrievably so."

The Reverend Lapp stood there, contemplating an irretrievably problematical hell while the great green globe of the world spun him about and the waters of the Meander were not spilled and the blue sky tucked its four corners down over Greenwillow. His eye observed with clear authority the worm in the blossom, the blight on the leaf, the devil in the dust, all of which would do most excellently for next Sunday's sermon.

"I cannot agree with you sir," said the Reverend Lapp. "I am quite certain about hell."

"That is your privilege," said Birdsong politely. They left it there.

Within a week's time, the strangeness of Providence which had produced two shepherds for the flock was agreeably adjusted by two church doors for the sheep, a mannerly solution thought up by the sheep themselves.

There was astonishingly little fuss. On Sundays the church

accommodated two sermons. The Reverend Lapp's voice rolled like thunder; the Reverend Birdsong's rolled like a cowslip ball. Lapp preached of a wide hell and a stalking devil, and Birdsong of a heaven as available as a pocket handkerchief.

Sometimes those who entered by the easterly, or Lapp, door would stay to heed the westerly sermon, as was the case with Little Fox Jones who came to hear Birdsong because he felt he needed a soothing ointment after the harangues of the Reverend Lapp. If Little Fox Jones had a fault, which he did, it was an overfondness for liquor that let him to take up residence so close to the village tavern that one had only to pull out the bung to find him. He was an ardent churchgoer, repenting every Sabbath, and for two in succession he listened to Birdsong, hopefully anticipating some new light on the Lord's intentions toward His incorrigible child. The experiment proved as unsuccessful as a cuckoo's nest, and Little Fox Jones went back to his earlier caretaker, with the Devil still faithfully at his heels and the hospitable coals of hell glowing through every bottle.

This defection left the Reverend Birdsong as untroubled as it had found him. He lacked Lapp's urgency and preferred to spend a large part of his time puttering contentedly about the woods and meadows where he composed his shapeless sermons. Like his pre-Witchett predecessor, he could not leave the river alone, and the villagers might have feared that he too would find a watery grave, had it not been so plainly evident that, under all circumstances, Birdsong would float.

Two clergymen in a single church quickly became an accepted thing. For comfort, one took Birdsong as one might take oil of cloves; for astringency, there was Lapp, bitter on the tongue but tonic for the system. Greenwillow attained an exceptional state of spiritual fortification.

Such then was the division of responsibilities that resulted, this particular September-gold morning, in the picture of the two clergymen following a single path. Their goal was half a mile down the river, first fork southerly, and about two catcalls down the road. This would bring them to the home of Amos Briggs, or rather of his family since Amos, that wandering man, could scarcely be said to have a home.

News that Amos Briggs had once more returned to Greenwillow had reached Birdsong and Lapp in the early morning, and they had both moved with creditable speed along the line of Christian duty. Lapp arrived at the river first, and Birdsong, sighting him, shouted an affable "Halloo." Lapp most unsociably pretended not to hear and broke into a canter, his long legs like black scissors in the high silver-wet grass.

"Halloo, halloo," cried Birdsong and ardently trotted after.

It took Lapp nearly a furlong of activity to realize that this was all most undignified for a man of the cloth, and he settled to a rapid walk. Birdsong had been rather enjoying the fine spectacle they must make, scuttling through the dew, but he was happy to slow down, and it was at this point of good cheer that he addressed the river as *fluvius,* causing, as has been remarked, a frown on the face of the Reverend Lapp.

Lapp was exceedingly anxious to be the first of the Lord's deputies to reach Amos Briggs. Predating Birdsong in the pulpit as he did, he had prayed a good deal more that Amos should see the light and return to his abandoned family, and now that these requests seemed to be bearing fruit he took it unkindly that Birdsong should reap profit where Lapp had sown prayer. He folded his hands in front of him, asking hastily to be redeemed from false pride, and loped along at an awkward angle.

As they left the river and turned southerly, a meadowlark showered the meadow with sudden song, and a large badger clambered out of a ditch and looked at them thoughtfully. Birdsong spun on his toes with delight.

This atmosphere of irresponsibility—the meadowlark scattering notes, the badger fraternal as badgers seldom are, the minister twirling—roused a sudden, deep-seated antagonism in Lapp. He said, and it was a warning, "Amos Briggs is a hasty-tempered man."

Birdsong ceased pirouetting and said meekly, "You know him and I do not. You shall lead and I shall follow."

Lapp decided there was much good in Birdsong and that it was in a meadowlark's nature to sing. "A hasty-tempered man," said Lapp, tuning himself pleasantly for a little lecture, "and wilful. A wanderer. Sometimes I fear he will always wander."

Birdsong cocked his head. "Blessed with five young ones, I believe."

"Six," said Lapp in a melancholy manner.

"Which would indicate," said Birdsong artlessly, "that Amos Briggs has at least returned at intervals."

This was a tender point, much harped on by Mrs. Lapp and sincerely deplored by her son, who now turned pink above the dignity of his collar. "At intervals," Lapp agreed shortly.

"Planting," said Birdsong sentimentally, "a little flower that you may water it at the font."

Lapp looked at him sharply, but the reverend's face was as innocent as a lamb's. Lapp's frown deepened. "It is not a laughing matter."

"Babies?" said Birdsong. "Oh, surely—"

"They are not babies. The youngest is three."

"It must have been a long wandering this time," said

Birdsong to himself, humming a little. "Happily, we can antici-
pate a new blossom next summer."

"Brother Birdsong," said Lapp severely, "you are affronting
the Lord."

"Dear, dear," said Birdsong, "I wouldn't want to do that."
He looked distressed for a moment, but a tangle of late traveler's-joy caused him to forget or at least mislay his sins. "I shall
give this to Mrs. Briggs," he said, plucking a handful. "One
should not come empty-handed."

It did seem to the Reverend Lapp that his companion was
being conspicuously pigheaded. It was not part of the church's
duty to bumble about with flowers, and anyway it was precisely that side of Mrs. Briggs's nature which should not be encour-
aged. He was about to remonstrate when the narrow track of
road they had been following took a sudden turn, shook itself
free of thistle and goldenrod and the autumn lace of spider-
webs, and deposited them in a circle of grass, a circle of trees
and a house in the middle with a crooked roof.

This was the farm of Amos Briggs, the wandering man, left
by him while he wandered and cared for by his young son,
Gideon in the summer heat and the winter cold and the pride
and growing of the little fields.

The gray house leaned east and its chimney leaned west and
a straggle of woodbine clawed at the windows. Two white geese
came hissing from the doorstep, and a tiny barefooted boy in a
cotton shirt of no decency whatever rushed out the door,
shouted furiously and rushed back again.

Of that wandering man, Amos Briggs, there was no sign
at all.

# CHAPTER TWO

GRANDMA BRIGGS had just mumbled her way through a large chunk of bread and drippings when the youngest, the smallest and in many ways the toughest of the Briggses beheld strange men in black descending on him, gave the howl which had heralded all his emotions from the cradle and plunged into the house to warn of something interesting in the way of devils and goblins.

"Shut up, mind y'r manners and sit down," said Gramma tartly, licking a film of grease from her old unsentimental claws. "Where's my turnip at?" She looked around for her daughter-in-law. "Girl, where's my turnip?" Thus had she addressed the first Mrs. Amos Briggs and thus she would address the second to her grave. Gramma was not good at names and she had forgotten her own maiden name decades ago. "Girl!" said Gramma with passion. "Where's my chawing turnip? They's people at the door."

Martha Briggs found the turnip where it had rolled under one of the beds and handed it over. Gramma took a bite and planted herself more firmly on the settle with her knees wide apart and her gnarled hands clutching the turnip, greedy and watchful as a squirrel.

Her daughter-in-law smiled placidly and nipped at her youngest's cheek with the backs of her fingers. Martha was broad-hipped and deep-bosomed with merry eyes and the look of a summer meadow, paying no more attention to details and with the same air of being touched by a fine clover-laden breeze. Her child nuzzled against her side like a little calf and felt very proud about living in a house with goblins outside.

"Who's visiting so early, baby?" said his mother.

"Black," he told her. "With hats on."

Gramma gave a squawk and nearly lost her turnip again. "Critters," said Gramma, "come to bury me afore I'm dead. I allus told you that's what would happen."

"Hush, ma," said Martha equably and put her child to ride on her shoulder where he drummed bare heels and bit at her hair. "It's likely just the two reverends from the church....Baby, where's all the rest of you?"

He gabbled, "Hustling the pig, bird nesting, helping Gideon. They wouldn't none of 'em let me go along. I'm gonna cry, ma. C'n I cry?"

"Sure, lovey." She let him slide down her back, over her hip and onto the cool dirt floor. "Get Gramma's turnip, it's loose again." She patted her hair and smoothed her skirt and smiled at her baby, and he gave up his idea of tears since the dog Rip had got hold of the turnip and was killing it in a dark corner. This was pleasant because Gramma knew her own chaw marks, and she was going to be in a simmer when she found out who had her turnip now.

Martha went to open the door and there the reverends were, just as foretold. Since the tall crowlike one was the Reverend Lapp, the round one with the clutter of blossom in his hand must be the Reverend Birdsong, whom she had not met before (being vague about Sundays, though not unchurch-ly). She smiled at them both.

"Mrs. Briggs," said the Reverend Birdsong, and gave her his traveler's-joy. She took it with true pleasure and stuck it into her bodice, upsetting the Reverend Lapp who considered this an impropriety, especially as Birdsong was prone to admire his gifts after bestowing them and, under the circumstances and location, this was going to be a very dubious project.

Lapp bowed cautiously.

Gramma gave a welcoming cackle and sprayed bits of turnip about her. "I'm real sorry," she said insincerely and point-ed at her vacant gums. "No chairs in the parlor."

"Eh?" said Lapp.

"No teeth, she means," said Martha. "Ma's got gums as hard as rock."

"Hard as rock, sharp as a blackberry thorn." Gramma regarded the visitors complacently. "C'd bite through a whole side of hog 'f I had a mind to."

"Reverends don't want to hear about your gums, ma," said Martha good-humoredly. "You got turnip spit all down your front."

"That's what God gave me my spit for," said Gramma.

This was not orthodox. The Reverend Lapp cleared his throat. "Mrs. Briggs," he said firmly, "I have come to call on your husband. I have come to rejoice with him that he has returned to the fold and to pray with him for surcease from his wanderings."

Martha sat down on a three-legged stool and laid her son comfortably across her knees, causing the insufficiency of his shirt to become more apparent than ever. "I'm real sorry you had the trip, Reverend Lapp," said Martha. "Amos didn't stay but the one day and the two nights. He's on his way again."

"You mean he has abandoned you again?"

"On his way," said Martha, nodding. "We had a real nice visit, and I reckon he's started another young un." Her mouth curled at the corners like the horns of a crescent moon.

Lapp gave a low cry. Birdsong said happily, "We explored the possibility on the way as we walked. I foresaw a summer baby in the baptismal font."

" 'Bout June," said Martha contentedly. "Seems like the cradle's been empty so long."

The Reverend Lapp bowed his head in his hands. Gramma regarded him interestedly. "Pain in your stummick," she suggested. "Know what's good for a pain in your stummick, Reverend?"

A hollow voice issuing between the clergyman's fingers said that he did not have a pain in his stomach, a statement which had no effect on Gramma. "Assafetty, whisky and rock sugar," she said, smacking her lips. "Raised me on assafetty, whisky and rock sugar, they did, and lookit me now. C'd chaw through the side of a hog." She seemed disposed to start the whole alluring discussion over again, and Birdsong, seeing a look of real pain cloud his colleague's brow, said hastily, "A fine little boy you have there, Mrs. Briggs."

Martha smiled, absently patting her child's bare bottom. "Present from Amos last time he was home," she said. "Says now he'd've give me twins if he'd knowed it was going to be so long atween. He went to Chiny this wander, I think. Takes a boat a long time."

"Indeed," said Birdsong. "China!"

The Reverend Lapp, who had raised his head from his

hands, put it back again. China was full of heathens.

"Chiny," said Martha, polishing the word. "So Jabez here is near three afore his pa come home."

Lapp reappeared. "Jabez?" he said hopefully. A Bible name, upright and of good behavior, was a favorable sign. He tried to remember what he knew about the original Jabez.

"Named from the Holy Book, all of 'em," said Gramma. "Amos is just like his pa afore him, can't stay in one spot and names all the young uns from the Holy Book. Micah and Bathsheby and Shadrach and Obadiah and Jabby here. Gideon was named from the Holy Book too, but Gideon had a different ma." She looked sharply at Martha. "Was her and Amos married, girl? I don't recollect."

"Yes, you do, ma," Martha said gently. "Her and me, we was both married good." She turned to the visitors. "Died of a fever with her second baby, she did, while Amos was roaming. When he came back he found me here, looking after Gramma and his Gideon. Gideon was six when his ma died."

"It was Christian of you," said the Reverend Lapp, feeling that they were moving to a higher level.

Martha shook her head. "The baby died too, you know. Poor little thing, lived three days and then died 'thout even whimpering. Like a little wax appleblossom it was." She hugged Jabez against her and he yelped with delight.

"God rest its soul," said Lapp, unexpectedly touched by a baby so distant. He then inquired belatedly if it had been baptized and, on being assured that it had been in a state of consummate grace, he said "God rest its soul" again, relieved.

"Amen," said Birdsong.

Martha turned her head at the sound of hoarse singing outside the door. "There's Bathsheby now. Sheby, come in here.

We got people."

Sheby sidled round the door jamb, marigold head, round nose, eyes like speedwells. Her blue stare took in the clerical visitation and became deeply suspicious. She opened her mouth to howl but, beholding Jabez quite calm and him not yet three, her seven years' dignity overcame her and she stuck her finger in where the howl would have come out.

"Where's the others?" said her mother idly.

"Micah's with Gideon. Shad 'n' Obadiah's giving swill to the pig."

"You catched him," said Gramma approvingly.

"Stuck in the hedge on the way to the village," Sheby told her. "He squealed like a sinner."

Martha said quickly, "Beg the reverends' pardon, Sheby."

Sheby begged the reverends' pardon, quite understanding that it was presumptuous to speak of sin in the presence of experts. The Reverend Lapp arose and asked where he might find Gideon. "I'll take you," said Sheby, leaping.

"You shall take us both," said Birdsong demurely.

Mr. Lapp sighed in resignation. Jabez slid down from his mother. The dog Rip stretched both ends and yawned, and Gramma hoisted her skirt above her bony knees. "She's a good girl," said Gramma unexpectedly, but there was no way to know what good girl she was talking about, Martha, Sheby or some old unwary self.

They left her to her flighty thoughts and Martha saw them off the threshold. "Gideon's mowing the meadow," she said. "I take it very nicely for you gentlemen to have come."

"We shall pray for your comfort," said Mr. Lapp.

"It ain't lacking."

"That your husband may see the light," said Mr. Lapp

patiently, "and follow his duty."

"He'll follow what he's a mind to," Martha said, "being a wandering man. You was never a wandering man, was you, Reverend?"

"God forbid," said Mr. Lapp, who was never allowed out of the house on a wet day without his heavy boots. He bowed austerely to Mrs. Briggs and led the processional as far as the corner of the house where Sheby skipped out front, bare-toed and slippy-footed but stern with the responsibility of guidance.

A tail flickered behind a hollow log and the dog Rip, who had been sniffing and sauntering, exploded into hunter, with Jabez howling behind. Sheby muttered, "He'll fall inna frogpond" darkly, but she let them go and held the Reverend Lapp in line behind her heels.

Birdsong they kept losing to the multitude temptations of summer's end: ripe plums on a shrunken old tree, their bloom pitted with honey-points; a far-off wagtail trying to fit two notes together; a haw, black and wrinkled and tasting of sun. When he brought back a field mushroom and offered it to Sheby, she took it silently and would not admit herself conquered but she kept looking backwards to make sure that, in his harkings and scuttlings, he did not fall into a rabbit hole.

When they came near the little meadow, they could hear Gideon's scythe singing and the silky whisper of tall grass dropping down, and the late grasshoppers talking around the edge. The scent followed the scythe, the hot oven smell of yellow turning brown, the dusty-powder smell of clover, the sharp smell of bruised pennyroyal like a plume in the air and, through it all, under it and around it the twitter and scoldings of small things being dispossessed and the hush-lullaby of the blade.

The grass falling behind him and the grass standing ahead,

Gideon moved and reaped, and at his heels Micah followed, gathering clumsily, gathering wrongly and with great good will, stopping to poke his bundle of gleanings, to fidget, to examine and to talk. He talked incessantly, they could see him talking by the bobbing of his cornsilk head, and then they could hear him as they came near, tirelessly out-chirping the grasshoppers.

Sheby hollered. Gideon let the scythe finish its curved flight and drop hook and turned to wait for the visitors, his dark head bent a little as if he was listening to their footfalls. Micah's mouth became an O of wonder and curiosity, but he was three years older than Sheby and would not give her the satisfaction.

"Here is the reverends, Gideon," said Sheby hospitably. "They've come to pray over you."

"A lovely meadow," said Birdsong, and sank into its lap.

"I don't need prayin' over," Gideon told them and frowned so that his brows made a straight black bridge above his eyes.

"No, indeed," said Birdsong cheerfully. "It wouldn't be proper unless you asked us to."

This was so completely untheological an approach that the Reverend Lapp gave a cry of pain, leading both Micah and Sheby to the pleasurable conclusion that he had been stung by a hornet. Micah's silence burst its buttons.

"They's a hornet nest down by the ellum tree, they's terrible late a-swarming. Person c'n die of a hornet sting 'thout you put mud on it." Micah looked wildly about. "Where's mud in a meadow?" he said, burying the reverend in the wink of an eye—poor reverend, dead of a hornet sting in a bright dazzle of September-dry.

"Hush up," said Gideon, cuffing him mildly. "Gentleman ain't stung." He looked at the Reverend Lapp.

Mr. Lapp's emotions were too complicated to be explained,

and Birdsong, oblivious, had found a little green snake in the long grass and was playing with it. Lapp gave him a hard look and turned back to Gideon. "We have come to pray with you," he said.

Micah said, "What we prayin' about?" and prepared himself at once in the attitude of one who is ready to receive.

Micah might be difficult to quiet but he was fallow ground for the mustard seed that the Reverend Lapp was finding so hard to dispose of. "For your father," he said.

"Pa's gone again."

"Cursed," said Lapp, "with the curse of wandering" and did not see how Gideon looked.

Birdsong let the little snake go.

Lapp said, "We wished to offer you the consolations of the church—"

"—and our help as neighbors," said Birdsong.

It had been the Reverend Lapp's intention to draw for Gideon a picture of the hell into which Amos Briggs would descend unless he had the prayers of the saved who stayed at home and did not ship for China, but he was unsettled by the momentary conviction that, if the Devil had got hold of any-body, he had got hold of the Reverend Birdsong. The briefest recollection assured Mr. Lapp that this could not be so, but again his ordered thoughts had fallen into grievous disarray while his colleague rocked on a meadow.

"We c'n do without your help," said Gideon ungraciously. "Soon now, things'll be so Micah c'n take over. Ma'll be able to manage by herself. When my call comes—"

"Your call?" said Birdsong.

"Like it come to Pa," said Gideon. "When I can't stay no longer, when I have to go."

"*You* would leave your family?" Reverend Lapp's fingertips came together, seeking out the shape of prayer.

" 'Tain't of my choosing. My father is a wandering man, Reverend, and his father and his father's father and all the ghosts afore 'em. I'll be a wandering man too."

"But the children—"

"He left *me,*" said Gideon, "and I fared. He left my own ma."

"And she died," said Mr. Lapp.

Gideon shook his head angrily. "It won't be that way when I go," he said. "I won't be leaving things the way my pa left 'em. I'm working and everything's growing, we've got geese now and a pig and, come next month—"

"Gideon!" shrieked Micah. "It ain't for telling. It's a secret!"

"It's not a secret any more, Micah, it's sure now." He touched his stepbrother's shoulder. "You c'n tell 'em, 'f you want."

Munificence nearly felled Micah; it did, in fact, make him silent for two breaths. "Cow," said Micah, spilling the news like a shower in drought. "Cow's a-coming to make her home with us, God's cow and Mister Clegg's." He threw in the religious thought from a desire to please the company, and it rattled the Reverend Lapp so much that he missed a crucial point.

Birdsong, however, did not. Thomas Clegg was eighty-nine or ninety-eight or a hundred-and-two or thereabouts, and he clung to life as he clung to everything he owned. His thin little wife patched him up and followed him about, scolding and nattering like a wren, and he clumped around his land or sat in the sun with his chin on his cane and his eyes rheumy from looking at what he owned, and no one had ever heard that he gave away so much as the hour blown off a dandelion-clock.

"Mister Clegg?" therefore said Birdsong.

"Cow with the staggers," Micah said, innocently explaining

much. "Gideon's to give Mister Clegg most of her milk and all of her calf if she gets around to calving. Takes a bull, you know," he said to the Reverend Lapp, feeling a sudden affection for the tall reverend, so nice and black and skinny. "You know it takes a bull to make a calf?"

The Reverend Lapp said faintly that he did know this, and he thought of his decorous home and he thought further that, when he reached its haven, he would sit in the parlor and close the shutters all around him. Even if it wasn't Sunday, even if his mother did object.

Birdsong said to Gideon, "You are to take care of Thomas Clegg's cow all through the winter? And then you are to give him most of the milk and let him keep the calf?"

"We've a shed," said Gideon, "and fodder. And I like cows." He leaned over suddenly, picking up a long stem of meadow-grass, running it through his fingers. "I don't think it's staggers she's got. It's her stomach is sour."

"Assafetty, whisky and rock auger," said Birdsong, nodding his head, and was delighted when Gideon smiled. Some sea wall ancestor, coming from nowhere, going on to anywhere, had passed too dark a hand across the young man's face, leaving the shadow behind. Birdsong hummed a little, pleased because light had fallen across shade.

"Gideon," said Mr. Lapp, sorely distressed, "you must not leave your family. You must wrestle with the Devil, you must pray for strength to see your duty—"

" 'Tain't of my choosing," Gideon said again. "A man's born to wander, he dies wandering. But I'll leave a good farm when I go."

"The Devil wanders," said Micah, meaning nothing, poetically fitting two words together to see if they became each other. "The Devil wanders on the sea and on the land, he wanders in Indy and Chiny and all them places my pa's been. He wanders afar and he wander near. I saw the Devil oncet."

"Oh, you did not!" said Sheby, wild with jealousy.

"Hush," said the Reverted Birdsong, penitently aware that he had already given Lapp a difficult morning.

But the Reverend Lapp was strongly in his own land now; the Devil had been invoked. Feeling the meadow abruptly his, he drew himself up and stretched out his hands. "The gates of hell are as wide as the world," he said, "and as narrow as a man's life. Kneel with me, Gideon. Kneel and pray to be delivered from wandering."

"I'll leave things in order," Gideon said. "But I'm marked for a wanderer, and I'll wander till the day I die, like my pa."

"Kneel!" Mr. Lapp thundered. "Kneel and pray!"

"My pa kneeled," said Gideon, "and he went away whistling."

The Reverend Lapp's hands dropped to his sides, and his face turned stony with anger. Pa's whistle could almost be heard in the distance, far away and careless as a mockingbird.

Birdsong got to his feet with difficulty, the grass entangled in his shoes. He said pacifically, "Your father came back, Gideon, you must remember that. He came back to his wife only two days ago."

"For a day and two nights," said Gideon with bitterness. "Pa can't help the call that comes to him," he said, "but he needn't have raised him a house and got him a wife and a family when he knowed he'd be leaving all behind, like his father and his father's father and—"

"—and his father before him and all the ghosts," said Birdsong resignedly. "Yes—well—"

"I'll go my way alone," said Gideon. "I'll not wed. Not ever."

# CHAPTER THREE

DORRIE FITTED the tarts into their tiny pans and tucked each one full with a dollop of gooseberry preserves before she gave it a pastry hat. With their middles rounded and their edges pinched, they looked like little haycocks, but Dorrie thought perhaps they were too small and shook her head at them.

Miss Maidy liked them small. Miss Emma, though she doted on pasties, would fold her hands and purse her lips when the tarts were passed to her, no matter what size they came. She would say no to them quite firmly, with a look from the corner of her eye that said, "Oh, the little dears!" and then she would take just one, very cautiously. The arrangements inside Miss Emma were understood to be very difficult, while with Miss Maidy it was her bones which required footstools and shawls and fine discussions about every breeze that trailed through a window.

The brindled cat came out from under the table to step into the oven with the little pies, and Dorrie boxed his nose for him. He smiled at her and sat down to comb his long fine whiskers, watching her slantwise. He was fat with cream and sleek with stroking and too lazy to catch even a slow-moving mouse, but Miss Maidy and Miss Emma excused all his weaknesses on the grounds that he had fits. They felt this must be very trying to a noble nature.

"Bad puss," said Dorrie and whisked the gooseberry tarts into the oven, from which there came shortly a smell of hot summer as the gooseberries burst their jackets and little sugar circles trickled down onto the goldening pastry.

Dorrie glanced out the door and saw that the sun was high, the air shimmering a little and the neat garden painted bright with yellow marrow and a cloud of flowery moths rising up over the phlox blossoms.

Miss Emma and Miss Maidy had gone off under their parasols to call on Mrs. Likewise, leaving Dorrie to mind the house as they had been leaving her for nine years now, almost since the first day when she came to Greenwillow, a sickly kitten of a seven-year-old. They had taken her in and fussed over her and cared for her and loved her, not even knowing then how well she could scrub and bake and shine. Not caring if she could do anything handy, it seemed, and that had astonished her.

Now she remembered very little about how she had come, a found child, running away from somewhere in the world outside beyond the Meander river. She had lived in a Home, she thought, but she was not sure and nothing of it stayed in her mind except a remembered smell of sour bread and the sound of neglected children humming to themselves in corners.

For nine safe years she had been in Greenwillow, sleeping nights in her own attic room with its little round window and its far corner where the floor met the roof, one walking crazily up and the other falling slantily down. The whole house was full of such sudden turns and fallings-about and little crannies that dirt might have liked to poke into, but no dirt escaped Dorrie and the spiders had given up their housekeeping entirely.

Puss said "Mow" and dusted his whiskers around her bare feet till she took a broom to his tail and he went out in the garden and sat under the sun. Dorrie, with the broom come to her hand quite by chance, used a yellow leaf as an excuse to sweep all the kitchen floor, and then she heard Puss speaking loudly and looked out to see Miss Maidy and Miss Emma coming sedately down the road.

Dorrie ran for her shoes behind the door and pulled at her braids that came down to her waist and shook out her gray cotton skirt and was at the front door, as neat as two pins, by the time Miss Maidy called from down the path.

"Dorrie, Dorrie!" Miss Maidy fluted, struggling in a subdued manner with the catch on the garden gate. Dorrie came running and pushed up the latchet and slippered Puss out of the way, he having strolled around from the kitchen side along with the delicate sniff of air that carried the scent of hot gooseberry tarts.

"Ah," said Miss Emma, clasping her hands. She was taller than Miss Maidy and thinner, and her nose being longer it was quicker to catch the tidings from the oven. Miss Maidy was a little like one of her own pincushions, of which she had nine, seven embroidered and two with lace.

"It's gooseberry tarts," said Dorrie.

"Gooseberry tarts," said Miss Emma, feeling the whole thing very deeply. "How I wish I dared—No." She turned to Dorrie. "Mrs. Likewise had currant cakes and all the currants had gone to the bottom. If it were not for being mannerly—" She sighed a little.

"I do think Puss is looking well," said Miss Maidy. "The

autumn agrees with him. Don't you think he's looking very well, Dorrie?"

"Yes'm," said Dorrie.

"We must go into the parlor," said Miss Maidy. "Mrs. Likewise had the most exciting news." She sobered her face, crumpling all its soft little lines and puckers to parlor sobriety. "Very *grave* news, of course. It has distressed the reverends. Mrs. Likewise told us only in the greatest confidence. Dorrie, dear," she said impatiently, "shan't we go into the parlor?"

Puss went in ahead of them to take Miss Maidy's special chair and had to be routed out, making a great scene and stalking up and down the carpet. Miss Maidy's shawl had vanished, and it became necessary to shut the latticed window, but the window had not been shut since the last sudden bright storm had drenched Greenwillow and, in the meantime, a vine tendril had crept in and was waving blindly about the parlor air, seeking something to grasp. The window could not, of course, be closed in a visitor's face, so the shawl must be found and this was accomplished only by much running about on Dorrie's part and a series of short anxious cries from the sisters, such as might come from parent robins having difficulties with the nursery.

Dorrie found the shawl under a pillow at last. Then, with the shawl placed and the footstool placed and Miss Maidy placed, she sat down on a spindly-legged chair, folded her hands politely in her lap and waited to hear the news that had distressed the reverends.

Miss Emma said suddenly that she felt a weight on her chest and that she feared it was Aggie Likewise's currant cakes. It was just possible that a pot of tea, cunningly steeped, might relieve her. And, if Dorrie was about in the kitchen anyway, she might just bring a very small gooseberry tart back with her for Miss Emma to toy with. Their dear mother had often declared that gooseberries were medicinal. "The juice, you know," Miss Emma said firmly.

Dorrie arranged it all with a white napkin spread on the tea tray and a hen-cozy over the pot. The hen-cozy had been crocheted four years earlier by the Reverend Lapp's mother, and it had come into Miss Maidy's hands at the church's twelve-month-giving. Every time Mrs. Lapp came to call, she would point out some new sign of deterioration in her creation and imply that it was not getting the best of care. This was very trying for Miss Maidy, who was exceedingly fond of all God's little creatures and had certainly proposed to do well by the hen.

There was no Mrs. Lapp about to complain today, and the gooseberry tarts, intended for supper, were a splendid success though their time was short. Dorrie watched with anxious affection while they disappeared and the little thin cups were emptied of their tea. Then Miss Maidy sighed with ladylike repletion and said, "Well, my dear, it seems that Mr. Amos Briggs has come home."

Dorrie knew all about the Briggses and it was common enough for the kitchen door to be favored by a small Briggs, come on business such as the barter of a goose egg. Micah or Sheby (or even Shadrach and Obadiah, though they were no more to be trusted with an egg than a mouse with a milkweed pod), each would stand at the door and sniff the good smells, golden and crusty when the bread loaves were baking or savory with marjoram and thyme in a bubbling pot or rich with fruit and sugar coming up through little pastry-holes like tiny windows.

They never begged, not even Micah. He would just stand about, looking wistful, with his nose nibbling at the air like a rabbit's, until Dorrie would sit him at the table and give him a bit of whatever-it-was. She never held with special hours for eating and nothing ever cooled without a knife slice in it.

"And now Amos Briggs has gone off again," said Miss Emma, moving the folds of her black silk to reclaim a flake of pastry. "The Reverend Lapp says it's the Devil's doing. We met him on the way home, Dorrie."

Dorrie put her elbows on her knees and her chin on her fists and stared, gray-eyed and interested. It did seem hard on Mrs. Briggs that she should have wedded a wandering man, and hard on Gideon too, left with a farm and a fistful of kinfolk. Dorrie had met Gideon seldom and then only when she happened near his meadow, searching out the field flowers that Miss Emma and Miss Maidy liked best, and she always felt shy looking at his dark serious face. Once there had been a citron bun in her pocket, brought to munch under a may tree, and she would have liked to share it with him. If he had sat under a may tree for a bit and eaten a citron bun, he might not have looked so terribly serious.

"He only stayed a day and two nights, Dorrie," said Miss Maidy.

Dorrie nodded. There would likely be a baby again in the Briggs's cradle, and small things in nesting places, like a cuddle of kittens in a haymow, had great appeal for Dorrie.

"And now he has gone, dear only knows where," said Miss Emma, "and Reverend Lapp will be preaching about him on Sunday. They're going to have a cow."

Dorrie thought for a moment that the cow was coming as a direct reply from heaven to the reverend's sermon but Miss Emma explained that the cow was Thomas Clegg's cow and she really did not know how such a thing had been arranged. "It would only be Christian," said Miss Emma, "to take our milk now from Amos Briggs's poor abandoned family. I expect it would be the same cow we have had all the time."

Dorrie said, "Miss Emma, they'll be the ones wanting the milk. With a baby coming, likely."

Miss Emma jumped, and Miss Maidy gave a little cry. Miss Emma said "Good heavens, child!" as soon as she had her breath back, and Miss Maidy said "Whatever do you suppose—?" and turned quite rosy.

There was a very difficult silence. Dorrie gazed penitently at the floor and was glad she had remembered to put her shoes on, one impropriety being enough. After a while Miss Emma said bravely, "Well, child, in our own parlor perhaps, but, my dear, you must not—it is so very—I mean, we don't know, we simply don't *know*."

Miss Maidy added, with the best intentions, that it would be so sad with Mr. Briggs in India (or was it China?) and Miss Emma looked at her sister very firmly and said with absolute finality that she feared Puss must have been eating grass again. "He wheezes," she said.

Dorrie got up and took Puss in her arms, burying her abashed face in his fur. He growled softly, but kept his pads curled and his claws demure inside them. Together they slipped out of the room, two shadows, one purring.

Behind them, Miss Emma said happily, "I doubt if it even occurred to Aggie Likewise, or she would certainly have said something."

Miss Maidy looked alarmed. "Sister! Dorrie is far too young."

"Nonsense," said Miss Emma briskly. "Dorrie's growing up."

41

# CHAPTER FOUR

OCTOBER FROST turned the meadow black. The
pig grew restless and the big gray badger who lived in
the woodlot closed his door and settled down,
grumpy with sleep and not giving thought to the spring that
would wake him.

On the great day of Mr. Clegg's cow, Micah woke before
dawn and wove his way around his sleeping family—Gramma's
mutter and Jabez's cluck—to go outdoors where he could
shout, unheard except by one pale star.

When Gideon opened his eyes, he missed the warmth of
Micah on one side of him, and after he had thought about
things for a moment he got up and dressed. It was not only
Micah's absence that routed him but there was the shed to be
given one more look. He and Micah and Sheby had scrubbed
it inside and clayed the chinks and spread hay, and Sheby, pressing a sweet meadow of timothy into the feedbox, had asked if
the newcoming cow would like two geese for company. "They
peck," said Micah, who had roused their ill will so often that
they now hissed at him without reflection like bowing to a
Sunday neighbor. "They'd be warm with the cow," said Sheby.

Gideon said no, the cow was to rest easy.

When he reached outdoors now, the little farm looking big and mysterious between moon-down and sun-up, he gave an asking whistle and Micah answered from the top of the shed where he sat, black against an apple-green sky, with his toes bare and cold because he had no time to find his shoes. Micah had very escaping shoes.

Gideon climbed up beside him, and Micah stretched out flat and beat the roof with his happy hands. "We'll go to Mr. Clegg's," he shouted, "and we won't take Sheby, and we'll bring our cow home with a ring in her nose and—"

"No ring," said Gideon.

"Where'd I get the idea they was allus a ring?" said Micah. "Somethin' has rings."

"Bulls," said Gideon.

"Bulls," Micah agreed, appeased, sitting up and pushing his cold toes under Gideon. "We don't lead her home by the ring in her nose, that's true enough. We lead her home by a little bit of rope which I am a-going to braid. Sweet cow." He snuffed the cold of the dawn and licked at it with his tongue. "Gideon, c'n I milk her?"

"Later, when she's peaceful in her stomach." He put an arm around Micah's shoulder and pulled him close, and Micah thought he could smell hay and apple on Gideon's shirt and wondered where the apple came from, the windfall not down yet and the hanging apples being for trade in the village.

"Micah," said Gideon, "you'll run the whole farm some day."

"When you go," said Micah, who had been chewing on when-Gideon-goes since the day he turned five and put on britches. "When will that be now?" There was no more in his asking than the liking for a twice-told tale.

"When I'm called. Maybe tomorrow, maybe two years away." Gideon's eyes were very dark. "Maybe one."

Tomorrow was impossible. Two years was forever, one year was half of two. Half of forever is a distant date, and even twelve months is too many to count on one set of fingers. Micah hugged his knees and rocked and was as comfortable as a chipmunk because forever was so long away. "It's sad you have to go wandering, Gideon," he said, "Here's so pleasant."

"You know I'd not go if it was my choosing, Micah," Gideon said longingly, and then added after a moment, "But you'll take care of things."

"Oh, I'll take care," Micah assured him. "Most I'll take care of the cow. I'll lead her to the meadow in the morning and I'll—"

"Likely she won't be here then. She's only a lend." Gideon stretched himself and looked at the dawn and knew there would be no fog today like there had been lately, coming white as a ghost, pressed against the house like a hungry cat. He wanted all the fair autumn he could get, putting things to rights even faster than he had planned to. It was Pa coming home that had done that to him, Pa only staying the one day and the two nights even though he'd wanted to stay longer. Pa had prayed on his knees against the wandering but his prayers were never answered, because if a man is called to be a wanderer nothing can stay him. And, like Gideon had told the reverends, Pa had gone away whistling.

"Ma's up," said Micah.

Gideon saw smoke curl from the chimney. The door burst open, and Sheby, Shadrach and Obadiah spilled out, followed by a howl from Jabez who was seldom where he hoped to be.

Sheby's eye flew to the roof of the shed like a cliff swallow to its hole, and she gulped with relief, having harrowed herself up with the notion that Gideon and Micah had gone by their lone selves to fetch the cow. Had this been true, her revenge on Micah would have been prodigious, but Micah on the roof could be regarded with charity. Sheby yelled at them that Ma was stirring the porridge kettle and that there would be raggedy-cakes to help celebrate the cow.

Micah soared from the shed top, arms flapping like a scarecrow. Gideon slid to the edge and dropped over. Sheby butted her head against him and said, "When we goin' for the cow, Gideon?"

"You ain't going," Micah told her.

Sheby shrieked. Shrieking, she leaped up and down. Micah shrieked back for her to hush, but she would not hush, even when Jabez careened out of the house, threw his arms around her knees and burst into tears. Gramma came teetering to the door and took in the scene, snuffling with the cold air and scouring her nose with the back of her hand. "Just like me when I was a un," said Gramma darkly. "Bad blood."

Gideon said "Sheby," and Sheby ceased. "We're all going for the cow," he said. "You and everybody. Even Jabez."

Sheby fell on her knees and embraced Jabez and they wept down each other's necks in a comradely fashion.

And that was how it was. They all went to get the cow.

Thomas Clegg was waiting for them, sitting on a fallen log, old as a leaf in winter, his shawl about his shoulders. They came in line cautiously, with Gideon ahead and Jabez last, and the children's eyes darted as fast as the tiny tongues of grass snakes.

Gideon said "Mister Clegg" respectfully, and Thomas Clegg

grunted and looked on them all with disfavor. Jabez commenced to wail, and Thomas Clegg gave a short laugh. "Never knew a child yet could abide me," he said complacently, drawing his shawl a little tighter against the October sun, and looked at Gideon bleakly. "Well, speak up."

"We've come for the cow," said Gideon.

Thomas Clegg rubbed his hands together with a dry rasping sound. "You keep her through the winter," he said, "and give me half her milk. She has her calf, I get it. That's understood."

Gideon nodded.

Thomas Clegg eyed him sharply. "Bred her to the traveling-bull, I did, late hawthorn time. Told you that, didn't I?"

Gideon nodded again. Micah and Sheby clasped hands in awful delight. They had seen the traveling-bull just once, when he broke free from his owner and stood, head down, black and monstrous in a sunny flower-filled meadow, snorting and bellowing and with fire coming out from his mean little eyes and lightning from his pawing hooves. It had taken three men to huddle the bull again and Micah and Sheby had been almost sorry for the great strong thing, goaded with pitchforks and an iron hook.

"Slipped her first calf," said Thomas Clegg, his eyes narrow. "Told you that too, didn't I?"

"Yes," said Gideon.

"Being straight and fair with you, ain't I? All's understood, ain't it?" He spat. The children were not impressed. Gramma could spit further and often did, even if the wall was in the way. "If all's understood," said Thomas Clegg, "you c'n go to the barn and lead her out. Don't take that passel of kin along with you. Other cows've got a right to their peace."

Gideon left him, with the children lined up staring and Thomas Clegg staring back like frogs in a swamp. The barn was warm and full of shadows and smelling of good hay and dung, and he could hear the shuffling in the stalls as the cows moved, listening to him. A hen cackled, talking up fussily about an egg she had been making. Gideon thought it would be nice to have a flock of hens and maybe a rooster to wake the sun. Micah would care for them, and Jabez could help hunt the eggs.

He stepped across the stone floor of Thomas Clegg's barn and spoke softly to all three cows.

The two in the near stalls turned their heads and stared with a large gentle gaze, switching their tails, but the far cow waited with her head down and Gideon knew she was the one he was taking home. He went in to her saying, "So bossy so," and put his hand against her flank, feeling how hollow it was, ridged with the big bone sticking out too high. Cows were bony, but this cow was all bones. He leaned down and pressed her bag gently, thinking with satisfaction about Ma filling herself up on good milk before the baby came.

He figured, standing there. Ma would give birth in June, the cow in early March if Mr. Clegg's remembering about hawthorn time was somewhere near right. It would work out fine. He had made the bargain for the cow before they were sure of the baby, but somehow it seemed they had known there'd be a lodger for the cradle from the moment Pa came home.

He unknotted the halter rope and led the cow out, wishing the shed that was waiting for her was as sturdy-built as this barn. "She'll get company," he thought, and maybe she would like that, but then maybe too what she liked was cow company and not a clutter of young ones.

When they reached the clutter, the cow gazed at them with

mournful eyes, but when they swarmed about her and patted her thin sides and Micah called her "sweet cow" and Shadrach tried mightily to reach up to her horns, then the cow lifted her head and mooed and the sound was splendid to hear.

By the time the welcoming was done and they turned back to Thomas Clegg, he had gone asleep, sitting there on his log, eyelids shuttered down, head drooping on his chest, shawl slipping to the ground. Sheby adjusted it for him and then stood back and eyed her work critically against the time when Mrs. Clegg would come along and take him out of the full sunlight and into the dark parlor. Sheby, holding Jabez by his quivering hand, had once peered through the window at the Clegg parlor and she knew it for a spindly place with a Holy Book on the great table and little white mats on all the chairs. If Sheby had been Thomas Clegg, she would have liked it better to live on the log in the meadow.

They let the cow set her own pace going home, and it was a slow journey but very eventful with Micah and Obadiah and Shadrach running in circles about her, Jabez discovering from the rear that a cow's tail is not to be hung upon, and Sheby walking gravely by Gideon's side and weaving a wreath of asters. It kept falling apart in her hands but, for such a cow, even Sheby could be patient.

When they came to the white road that ran under the hill just before it forked to take them home, they also came to Little Fox Jones, sitting under a hedge, very cheerful and studying his toes. He watched them nearing with their lovely cow, and when they drew close he put finger to lips and said in warning, "He've just gone down the lane," but when they asked who "he" was he looked surprised and told them Mr. Lunny. This could not be true, because Mr. Lunny, who kept the tavern in the village, had a wooden leg and never stomped so far as this.

"It couldn't be Mister Lunny," said Micah.

"Here's a cow," said Jabez, suddenly ducking his head and pointing.

"So 'tis," said Little Fox Jones, seeing a large whitish thing and having no reason to believe it was other than a cow.

"She's ours," said Jabez.

"Lended to us," said Micah. "From Mister Clegg. He wedded her to the traveling-bull last hawthorn time and Gideon says she'll drop a calf in March. You heered of dropping calves, Mister Jones? I told the Reverend Lapp about it but he knowed already."

Little Fox Jones gave a happy cry. "That's who 'twas—the Reverend!" he said. " 'Twasn't Mister Lunny at all. He didn't have no wooden leg." He looked anxiously if a little foggily at Gideon. "Reverend Lapp, he don't have a wooden leg?"

Gideon said no, and Little Fox Jones gave a cackle of triumph. "No wooden leg, must be the Reverend. I recollect now, we prayed together." He recalled it with pride, saying, "We dusted our knees together, asking for my salvation. That's why I'm a-sitting here now, come to think of it. I'm waiting for my salvation to strike me."

Micah's mouth fell open, Sheby let her wreath slide from her fingers. The cow dropped her head, and Gideon leaned against her, rubbing her calm wide forehead. No one was in a hurry.

"It'll come as a ball of fire from the Angel of the Lord," Little Fox Jones said impressively. "A ball of fire, and a great sword a-carving up the sky." He held up a hand to warn them against any premature rejoicing. "That's if the Angel of the Lord comes, but Reverend says it ain't likely. Reverend says the Angel of the Lord don't keep his habitation at the tavern with Mister

Lunny. I don't know why," he added, forestalling Micah's question. "Mister Lunny's a good upright man, but it ain't the good upright men what comes to salvation, far as I can see. It's me what's goin' to be saved. Or not," he said thoughtfully, "as may happen."

Micah could contain himself no longer. "Comes no salvation, who comes?"

Little Fox Jones straightened up importantly. "Devil," he told Micah, "walking on cloven hoofs—"

"Like the traveling-bull," said Sheby, shivering with wonder.

"—flames of Hell burstin' about him, earth quaking under his feet. Darkness afore him and behind him and winds a-rustling. It's to be a fearful tussle."

"Who's tusslin' who?" said Obadiah shrilly.

"Devil's tusslin' the Angel of the Lord for my soul," said Little Fox Jones and turned to Gideon. "Comes to me now, Gideon," he said apologetically. " 'Twasn't the Reverend went by just now. Yesterday it were when he went by and I was sittin' here."

"Who was it?" said Gideon politely.

Little Fox Jones groped a moment, losing the name he wanted. Then, "Dorrie!" he said triumphantly. "Dorrie from the village. Drivin' a pig and goin' your way."

"Driving a pig?"

"Drivin' a pig." A slight irritability at being questioned came over Little Fox Jones. "And goin' your way. You'll catch her up likely, the rise of the hill, which you'll be wanting to do. The position being," said Little Fox Jones in a very dignified manner, "that I'd a known that pig in the deeps of hell itself— clipped ear, white foreleg and a snout like a alligator."

The gates of hell receded, the Angel of the Lord sheathed

his sword, and the torn heavens came together before the urgency of this news. Little Fox Jones's listeners cried, "That's *our* pig," in one mighty voice, and the procession took shape and abandoned him with such speed that even the cow was roused to an ungainly trot.

Little Fox Jones watched them disappear around the bend and shrugged. He moved to a place under the hedge where the sun could reach him and the breeze could not, and he settled down inside his coat like a hedgehog. A spider, finding him there, wove him into its web.

# CHAPTER FIVE

THE PIG was giving Dorrie trouble. It was an emotional pig and a wilful one and, whenever she poked it out of the ditch on one side of the road, it would dodge her crooked stick, squeal furiously and trot into the woods on the other side.

Dorrie kept making appeals to it and wishing someone else had found it, but this was hopeless wishing as it had appeared suddenly, rooting about in Miss Emma's vegetables. Miss Emma had cried out sharply and wrung her hands, and this provoked the pig so that it charged Miss Emma and cornered her in back of the crab apple tree. Miss Maidy, seeing all this, burst into tears, the pig being large, and Dorrie flew out of the kitchen and threw the empty slop pail straight at the pig's head.

The pig grunted and sat down backwards, and Dorrie tossed her apron over its head and shepherded the two ladies back into the house. By the time she came back the pig had turned philosophical and was wearing the apron like a sunbonnet and chewing on a cabbage leaf. Dorrie shooed it gently out of the garden, feeling already a little remorseful about the slop pail, and then ran back to tell Miss Maidy and Miss Emma, who were considerately fanning each other, that she would drive the pig home to the Briggses' farm. There was no question but that it was the Briggses' pig, it being a well-known animal about Greenwillow and subject, like Amos Briggs himself, to wandering.

Miss Maidy leaned out the parlor window, fluttering a cambric handkerchief and issuing good advice from a safe distance. "Do take care, Dorrie, it's in a terrible temper. Perhaps it has fits like Puss—Dorrie, where *is* Puss? Sister, have you seen Puss?" She gasped with this new affliction, cat devoured by pig, and sank into a chair. Puss got out of the chair just in the whisk of time and came to the window to examine the fuss. Dorrie said, "Nice puss. Come, piggy," and prodded the pig into an amble.

Miss Maidy, reappearing, waved them both goodbye and remarked to her sister on how brave Dorrie was, a thought she was able to pass on later to the Reverend Lapp who stopped by to inquire about their spiritual state. The pig and Dorrie's gallantry had both grown by that time, and the reverend took away with him an impression of flying banners and a herd of Gadarene swine.

It was a fine day for reverends being about, and Dorrie met Mr. Birdsong coming out of Mr. Preeb the baker's, where he had been fortifying himself with a rowdy-bun, Mrs. Likewise's sweets running to milk puddings which would better please her cats should any be left over. The rowdy-bun had been stuffed with jam and studded with currants and the Reverend Birdsong was licking sugar off his fingers when he met Dorrie.

He was exceedingly pleased, having a great fondness for her and calling her "my child" in the tenderest way since Dorrie had never owned a last name and was not quite anybody's child. He was mildly surprised that she had acquired a pig.

Dorrie said shyly that it was the Briggses' and that she was returning it. "Ah yes," said Birdsong, quite as if ferrying pigs about was a local custom. "Should you see young Gideon, give him my wishes." He eyed both Dorrie and pig affectionately and said suddenly, "My dear, would you have room for five kittens?"

"Five, sir?" said Dorrie anxiously.

"Well, about six, I think. That good woman Mrs. Likewise has a cat who is quite tireless. The kittens are all gray this time and just beginning to romp. I found one in my pillow last night, and this makes twenty-one in or about the house." He smiled at Dorrie. "I think Mrs. Likewise could be prevailed on to part with half a dozen if you could harbor them. All gray."

"Reverend, I don't think Puss would let me, or Miss Maidy or Miss Emma—"

"I'd forgotten Puss," Birdsong admitted. "We must try to influence him, then. If he agrees, Miss Maidy and Miss Emma will see it his way in no time. Thank you, my dear, I shall call. Some pie day I think. You know, I smell your pies coming over the hedge now that the leaves have gone. Dear, dear, I wish I had a flower for you." He lifted his hat to her and to the pig and was gone.

Dorrie poked the pig, who had been sitting quietly and eating a leaf. They went on through the village, down the road and up the fork after the bend, meeting Little Fox Jones just at the rise of the hill. He looked at them slyly but did not speak, and as the pig chose that moment to lurch into the ditch, Dorrie had little time for greeting.

They went almost in sight of the farm when she heard a cry of voices and looked back to see an army of Briggses, headed by a large cow. Dorrie had never seen the family all at once, and it took her a moment to sort them separately, so many and so various.

Micah came leaping and telling as he leaped. "Dorrie, we've a cow! She's to live in our shed and some day I'll milk her, we shall have cream. *How* did you come by our pig?" He tugged at her, jumping urgently, pointing out cow, pig, Dorrie in case any of them had missed each other.

The rest came up and Dorrie smiled at the children, a little unsurely, used to each as she was but not to the medley. When her eyes came to Gideon, she was surprised to find him so tall above her, and she looked down at the pig in confusion.

The pig was working up a terrible fury, little pig eyes piggier than ever as it squealed with rage. It was perfectly clear that the cow was the cause of the tantrum, and the cow resented this and gave an indignant moo. Gideon jumped and caught the pig just as it was about to depart forever. He hoisted it and held it tight against his side under one arm, and after a while it stopped fighting.

Gideon put it down on the ground where it stood, grunting a bit but mollified.

"Poor little pig," said Dorrie, quite forgetting all its misdeeds and Miss Emma's fright.

"He thought things were amiss," Gideon agreed. "It was good of you to bring him so far."

"He was in Miss Emma's garden," said Dorrie simply.

"Did he do harm?"

"Oh, no!" said Dorrie, shocked.

They stood looking at each other, and Micah, who did not believe that one moment of silence should ever be linked to another, said, "Dorrie, we're almost to home. Dorrie, come see us bed our cow." He pulled at her skirt, and she took his hand suddenly and said she would come, although she knew she ought to be turning back.

There was no more said and they started up the road once more, the cow in front and the pig trotting as dainty and refined as a Sunday bonnet. They had passed a stile and two frogs in a pool of ditchwater and a great white puffball, which Jabez sought to eat, and a fallen log that buzzed with hornets, before Gideon spoke again to Dorrie, though she had been waiting anxiously, fearful he might be vexed with her for coming. Maybe a stranger was not welcome at the bedding of the cow, and, unlike his kin, Gideon had never lingered in the kitchen doorway sniffing her oven. She thought of making a great pie only for him, and then she put the thought away because he was busy on his farm and could not come like the others. Nor would want to.

Gideon said, "Little Fox Jones said you had gone by."

"I did," said Dorrie, and added, "The pig was hurrying me," to explain why she had not passed the time of day.

Gideon nodded, and there was silence again and then Dorrie remembered that she had a message. "I met the reverend in the village," she said. Gideon stiffened and his black brows drew together. "Mr. Birdsong," said Dorrie and, though she did not know why his forehead smoothed out, she was pleased. "He sent you his wishes."

"It was kind," said Gideon and might have said more but just then Micah shouted.

"Cow, there's your shed," cried Micah, and everybody except Dorrie and Gideon began to run, fine sunbeamed dust floating up behind bare heels and hard hooves. From the house there came a clamor of barking, and Rip, who had been left home because his manners were very uncertain toward Mr. Clegg, rushed out. The pig, who had known Rip for years, gave a contemptuous snort, but the cow put her head down low and pointed her horns and pawed at danger.

There was a moment when the whole world teetered and even Micah held his tongue, but just in that moment Rip recollected having seen cows before and, instead of leaping on this one, he leaped on Obadiah. Obadiah gave a glad cry, simply because Rip usually favored Shadrach.

"Girl!" said Gramma's voice, hollering above the general din. "They's home."

Dorrie stopped short, feeling certain she had been wrong to come. No one had invited her, not really, excepting Micah and he was likely too young to know any better. "I should go home," said Dorrie, under her breath and very fast.

Micah seized her, twisting like a dodder vine, "The shed, Dorrie, the shed," he said anxiously. "Ma, here's Dorrie, she *must* see the shed. Ma, must she not?" He beseeched, quivering.

Dorrie might still have turned and been gone, but just then Martha Briggs came out on the doorstep, a being no more possible to disturb than a mill pond, and smiled at her and at the cow and at the children and Gideon.

Just behind her came Gramma, peeping like a witch and clutching her turnip. "Call that a cow?" said Gramma. "Swayed in the back and knocked in the knees. 'Twon't give us milk, it'll give us pizen water. Why'd Thomas Clegg lend her if she don't give pizen water?" She glittered her bright black eyes at Gideon.

He said, "She'll give sweet milk, Gramma, but you'll get none," and Gramma threw her head back and laughed like the girl she had once been. When she came out of the early gold cloud of her mirth, she caught sight of Dorrie and forgot the cow. "Who's that?" said Gramma, pointing.

"You know, Gramma," said Gideon. "Dorrie, from the village. She's brought our pig home."

Gramma said perversely. "Better have left it to die with its feet in the air. Where's the rest of your name, Dorrie-from-the-village?"

Dorrie stood silent.

Gramma gave one of her cackles. "Don't mind, child. Get you a man and you'll get you a name. That's what all the pussies do, that's what I did. Speak up, though. Devil got your tongue?"

"No, ma'am," said Dorrie.

Martha said, "Stop pestering her, ma. Come inside, Dorrie, and ease yourself. Pig gave you trouble, I suppose. Born to make trouble, that pig was. He was a giveaway runt and he always knowed it." She sighed pityingly. "Seems like animals do know, poor things."

Micah said pleadingly, "Don't go in the house, Dorrie. We want you to watch us bedding our cow."

Dorrie looked at Martha uncertainly, wanting so much to step over the threshold and through the door and inside the house. She loved houses from within, warm corners, sitting places, hearthfire, little patched things about, stew kettle bubbling maybe. It was a nice cow, of course, but all cows laid down on hay exactly alike.

Martha said, "Bed the cow, then come get Dorrie," and waved them all off like gnats, taking Dorrie and Gramma in through the door with her. "You'll have some broth?" said Martha.

"Please, ma'am," said Dorrie, sitting on the settle with her hands folded and looking about her.

Considering so many children and so much to do, Mrs. Briggs kept her house very well, but it was all Dorrie could do not to jump up and snatch the broom from behind the door.

59

The floor could never be scrubbed as a floor needed to be scrubbed, on hands and knees and aslosh with soapy water, because it was made of dirt, but it was as hard as rock and could be swept. The top gray dust would curl like smoke as she chased it out the door, and the brown good earth beneath it would look almost as neat as Miss Maidy and Miss Emma's wood floor, except for the gleam like a rubbed chestnut.

Dorrie stopped looking at the floor and looked at a corner. A spider was swinging from the roof, a tiny black clot coming down very slow and gentle as if it knew no one would trouble its journey. Dorrie frowned. She had nothing to speak of against spiders but outdoors was the place for their cobwebs. She watched while it tiptoed on long legs toward the stove and disappeared into a wall crack, and then there was the stove to fret her. There were three pots on it, with crusted bottoms and smoke-stained sides, and the stove's black face was no better.

It could be rubbed. It could be rubbed until it shone, and then the light from the hearthfire would gleam on it and the lamp when it was lit at night and everything would be warm and bright. She looked at the hearthfire, but it happened at the moment (the October sun being as ripe as a plum) that the fire was dulled to a few sparks and the ashes were dingy. A bundle of rags lay where there should have been a hearthbrush, and "Oh" thought Dorrie, a pain in her heart because the Briggs family had no brush for its fireside. At Miss Maidy and Miss Emma's, the brush had stout bristles bound in bright wool, and the hearth had tiles that were as clean as the best dinner plates with the roses on them.

And yet in their home there was only Miss Maidy and Miss Emma and herself, and here there were eight and maybe a ninth to come. She looked around a bit more and her eye came to the cradle, a little brown thing shaped as carefully as a cockleshell, and she gave a cry of delight and got up. She wanted to touch it with her hands.

There was nobody in it, of course, that would have to wait, just an old piece of blanket.

I could make a quilt, thought Dorrie, a little blue quilt out of the pieces Miss Maidy gave me. Would they mind, oh, would they mind if she made it a quilt? She darted a look at Gramma, but Gramma was half asleep, in her rocking chair, waiting for her broth to come.

"It's pretty, ain't it?" said Martha not turning from the stove. "Gideon made it, summers ago. Shadrach and Obadiah both laid in it, and Jabez too. Come June, there'll be another."

Gramma opened one eye. "Anybody can add knows that, girl. Where's my broth at?"

Martha gave her a full bowl, and Gramma disappeared into it with a noise like the Meander at flood time. Dorrie took her own bowlful and said shyly, "The new baby, Mrs. Briggs, do you think I might make it a little quilt?" and then she wished the words back because Mrs. Briggs might think she was disfavoring the old piece of blanket.

"Why, lovey," said Martha, touched. "Hear that, ma? Dorrie's making a quilt for the next un. None of the others had what you could rightly call a quilt. It would be—You really *want* to make it a quilt, Dorrie?"

Dorrie nodded, feeling happy. "I have the blue cloth, ma'am, and I like to sew."

"Better you than me," said Martha. "I never had the touch. I sew like a bramblebush, and Sheby's worse'n I am." She sighed unregretfully. "It's like feeding. I can fill their stummicks but I can't make a pie that makes you think of heaven."

"I guess nobody can," said Dorrie, smiling at the idea.

"Micah says that's how yours taste," Martha said. "He come home one day turning handsprings like a lamb in a meadow, singing like a bobolink. Said you'd gave him a piece. Gideon figured maybe he'd pay your kitchen a visit someday, hisself."

"He never came," said Dorrie, a little wistful.

"Oh, he never meant it serious," Martha said quickly. "Gideon's not one to ask . . . . Ma, you're blowing that broth right out on the floor . . . . He's prideful and that's a sin, but he's been good to me, Gideon has. Sun'll rise up dark for a while, I guess, after he's gone. But you get used to things, and Micah knows more sense than he shows. Gideon's taught him."

Dorrie put her bowl down carefully on the table. "Gideon's going away?"

"Got no choice," said Gramma, smacking her lips and looking around for her turnip.

"Oh, lovey, they all go away," Martha said a little wearily. "It's somethin' has to be lived with. Oldest son of the oldest son, each one marked, I guess, from the days of Adam hisself. Wandering men, all of 'em, and when their call comes they go."

"Their call?"

"That's how they name it," Martha said. "Amos said you could never mistake it, it comes so clear."

"Hoeing man lays down his hoe," Gramma put in, setting her son's story straight.

"That's right." Martha nodded. "Come to Amos in the field, it did, he put down his hoe and followed it then and there. It don't seem right to a woman, but you can't argue with a river where it's going or a rock where it will rise."

"But—" said Dorrie.

"Gideon frets," Martha said, "That's the only difference.

He's readied himself, like coming to baptism or somethin'. He's raised Micah to do what's got to be done and he's fixed things so's we can manage. I know in my heart that he'll go away sad, but he'll go, Dorrie, when his call comes."

"Amos goes whistlin'," said Gramma, and tried to do it for them toothlessly.

"Well," said Martha, putting it all behind her, "there's times he comes back too. Seems like a wandering man has to have a place to wander from."

There were five shouts from outside, chiming like bells. Someone cried, "Dorrie! Come quick, cow's bedded," and Dorrie ran to the door.

Micah was first and caught her hand and flew her to the shed. "She'll get up," he panted, "if we don't hurry," and then they were all at the shed and he thrust her through the doorway ahead of him and, sure enough, cow was bedded.

The cow seemed very surprised about it and well she might, for it had taken the strength of all the Briggses to make her lie down and appreciate her new comforts. She was a passive cow but she was also used to keeping her own hours, and this daylight bedding was new to her. Still, the hands were gentle and the hay smelled of clover and one place was very like another.

Gideon, down on his knees in the hay, looked up at Dorrie's shadow across the door. He held out his hand and said, "Come stroke her, she's easy in her mind now," and Dorrie crossed the little shed and kneeled beside him, not caring about her skirts.

"Rub between her horns," said Gideon, watching the cow. "She likes it, so," and he took Dorrie's hand and placed it to delight the cow.

Dorrie looked at his hand on hers and saw his sleeve which had been torn and mended, just as Mrs. Briggs said, like a bramblebush had done the sewing.

"Dorrie!" said Gideon anxiously, needing the cow to be praised.

"She's a lovely cow," said Dorrie. "Oh, Gideon, she's a lovely cow!"

# CHAPTER SIX

ALL SAINTS' DAY brought festival attendance to the little church with both its pastors in fine voice, but All Souls' Day brought a gale riding the November wind.

It tore the last yellow leaves off the great willow and cracked a branch so that it hung desolate above the Meander. It knocked the chimney off Mr. Lunny's tavern and whined all night, rattling shutters, wrenching open one of the church doors and screaming up and down the aisle, searching the startled pews and throwing hymn books about.

When it finally flung itself out against the sky and the sun came through a tatter of clouds, there was nothing much to show for the violent night except Mr. Lunny's chimney and the nervousness of Aggie Likewise's cats who seemed, for days after, to float about two inches above the carpet.

Puss, having had his fit the day before, when all was calm, slept the gale out in Miss Maidy's chair and ate the next morning more than ever before in the memory of man. Dorrie, coming downstairs, found him humped over an empty bowl, and he growled at her so that she gave him her own share of porridge before she went up to waken Miss Emma and Miss Maidy with tea. When she came down, Puss had licked his bowl clean again and was on the table and into the porridge pot, muttering through his whiskers.

Dorrie fed him all day long and still could not satisfy him, and for a while she thought he was not Puss at all but a cat-soul left behind from the celebrating. When he calmed at last and even turned up his nose at a bit of cheese, she was greatly relieved, and when he tried to get his head into the big crock which held the bilberry preserves, she knew him to be quite cured. Puss did not like bilberries and could only have acted in mischief.

The berries were for little cakes, and the smell of the hot fat things in the oven must have climbed the hedge and wafted down the road to the Reverend Birdsong. Dorrie scarcely had the first baking out on the table, wearing sugar caps and crisp at the edges, when the Reverend Birdsong came questing.

Dorrie was terribly upset. No one ever called at the back door, least of all a reverend, and her apron was stained with blue juice and her feet were bare and she had no time to run and hide. She tried opening the door just a crack and telling him that Miss Emma and Miss Maidy were at the Ladies' Meeting, but he was cheerfully deaf for the moment and came through the door like a squirrel looking for nuts.

"Bilberry cakes!" said the Reverend Birdsong. "How lucky I happened along just when I did. It must have been the Lord's will." He began to go through his pockets and bring out kittens while Dorrie watched, amazed, and Puss's tail grew rigid with rightful horror. "Samplings," said the Reverend easily. "All gray as I told you, but I thought you should see them before we took the matter up with the ladies. Ah, here we are." He got the last one out by its tail and it mewed and then stood up unsteadily on the table top among its relatives, a small puff of fur with eyes so blue that the bilberry cakes nearly cried out and Dorrie certainly did.

"That one," said the Reverend Birdsong, "yes. A kitten of great promise, but much in need of a home because of its paw." He held up the kitten in both hands and showed the front paw which had a limp pitiful look. "It passed through my mind that anyone partial to bilberries would like the kitten's eyes. *I* am partial to bilberries, you know," he said, sighing like an April breeze.

"Oh, Reverend," said Dorrie, aghast, and hurried to get him a plate and a napkin and a pat of golden butter to put just in the center of the cake where the hot sugary fruit would melt it. "I never minded you were hungry. I was so mindful of the kittens, I *am* sorry." She stopped one of the kittens from falling over the table edge, reached for a second, then a third, and finally scooped the whole lot up in her apron and piled them into the basket that stood ready for wood chips. The bilberry kitten came up over the side and hung by its chin and one paw, mewing. Dorrie lifted it out to hold against her cheek.

"Six," said the reverend, deep in his cake. "Or did I only bring you five?" He looked uneasy and half rose. "Could I be sitting on one?"

"That's the quilt for the cradle," said Dorrie, pulling the blue cloth out from under him and very glad her needle was safe in its folds. "It's for Mrs. Briggs's baby, and it's all but done. Just the blue ribbon still to be fastened at the top."

"Right here," said the Reverend Birdsong, being careful about his buttery fingers.

"Yes, sir. The ribbon's a gift from Miss Maidy, she took it off a pincushion when I told her what the quilt was for."

"A good lady," said the reverend, looking at the bilberry cakes in a thoughtful manner. "They're best eaten hot, of course."

Dorrie put the kitten back into the basket and Puss snarled at it. "Dear, dear," said the Reverend Birdsong, "how very unchristian." His hand crept out and hesitated above a small cake.

Dorrie said, "Sir, Miss Emma and Miss Maidy would want you to be sitting in the parlor, I think."

"We must settle the kittens first." He sighed. "I see now that Puss would never consent to six, but if you would take the lame one—"

She passed him the cake he had been watching and looked doubtfully at the basketful of fur. The door latch gave itself a shake, and Dorrie went to it quickly in case it should be Mrs. Likewise come after her lodger and her kittens. It was not Mrs. Likewise, it was Micah Briggs with a blue nose and his toes coming through his shoes and a willow stick in his hand.

"Pig's away again," said Micah, falling midstream into his news. "Gideon said likely it'd go faring to you, you was so kind to it last time for all it gave you trouble." He peered beyond her and saw the cakes and the reverend at the same moment. "Good afternoon, Reverend, I'm seeking for our pig. What's these?" He was distracted for a moment by the rustle and mew in the chip basket and by Puss's exclamation. "Cats and cats," said Micah delightedly. "Dorrie, how did you come by a basket of pussies? May I have one? May I have two?"

"You may have five," said the Reverend Birdsong. "The sixth is Dorrie's because it wants her, whatever Puss says."

"The lame thing," said Micah, "that would be Dorrie's. Is it true I can have all the others, Reverend, they's one for everybody almost. I could take them in the basket, Dorrie, I would bring it back at once. When I find the pig—You do know I have to find the pig first, don't you?" He looked quickly around the kitchen in a reliable manner and saw the cakes again. "It's hungry, hunting pigs," said Micah.

The Reverend Birdsong said, "Oh, certainly."

Dorrie gave him a cake, and it was followed by the miracle of Micah being silent but it was a brief miracle and lasted only while the Reverend Birdsong counted to twelve out of curiosity. "Cow's middling," said Micah, quite as if anyone had asked. "Time there, she wouldn't chew her cud, and Gideon, he was a-worrying. Cow must chew her cud or her horns'll curl up and she'll die a horrible death. Who told me that?"

"Not Gideon, I think," said the pastor gravely.

"Sheby told me." Micah put his elbows on the table and his chin in his hands and stared at another bilberry cake. "Little hole where the sugar ran about," he said critically. "See, Dorrie, how too bad, you'll hardly be wanting to give a thing like that to Miss Maidy or Miss Emma now, will you?"

"Butter's in the crock," said Dorrie, thinking about Gideon having trouble with the cow.

"Cat's very cross," Micah said, finding the crock with no trouble at all and digging so much butter from it that the Reverend Birdsong's eyes widened in unchurchly envy. "I'd best take all the kittens away but the lame one."

"Does she chew her cud now, Micah?"

Micah nodded. "Gideon, he gave her hay-tea and turnips. The turnips taste in her milk and Gramma likes it fine on porridge. Milk's still scarce in our cow, Gideon says she'll come down better when she's nestier. I've not been allowed to milk her yet, you know, Dorrie, and I wish I'd be allowed. Gideon goes, who'll milk her but me?"

Dorrie said quickly, "Micah, has his call come?"

"No, Dorrie. Ma's prayin' it'll not come afore June when the baby's going to be birthed. Call won't wait, you know." He sighed. "Reverend Lapp says Gideon is wilful. Says he won't humble his heart and loosen his knees and pray to be saved from the Devil's hold. Reverend Lapp says the call comes from the Devil."

"Has he been visiting you lately?" said the Reverend Birdsong curiously.

"Who? The Devil a-walking?"

Tempted, the Reverend Birdsong virtuously shook his head. "No, Micah, the Reverend."

"Reverend Lapp, yes, comes very often, very tall in his funny hat."

"It's the same hat I wear," said Birdsong fairly.

"Different somehow," Micah maintained, "him being higher up and all. Gideon won't go down on his knees, and Mister Lapp, he gets very dissatisfied."

"But that's not right, Micah," said Birdsong, looking troubled. "There's great power in prayer, and Gideon should be willing to seek the Lord's help."

"Oh, it's never the Almighty the Reverend prays to," Micah said, "it's the Devil. They's no use praying to the Almighty when it's the Devil what's after Gideon's soul. That's what Mister Lapp says anyway, and he's the one who's acquainted with Satan."

"Oh, dear," said Birdsong unhappily. "Does Gideon believe all this?"

"Well, Mister Lapp says Gideon is cursed," Micah pointed out, "and, if it's true, it must be the Devil's doing. I allus understood from Ma that the Lord was mightier than the Devil, but maybe this time the Lord sent the Devil and told him to go stalking up and down Greenwillow. Could that be?"

"Micah," Birdsong murmured, "you're making my head ache."

"Reverend Lapp says the Devil is surely abroad in the land."

"So is the pig," said Birdsong, mildly violent, "and you should be out hunting for it and taking those kittens home. Put them into the basket, Micah, and go hunt that pig before I fly out of my skin."

Confronted with this fascinating possibility, Micah became almost immovable. It was Dorrie who basketed the prowling kittens and thrust them at him along with one last bilberry cake. "Tell your ma I'll be bringing the quilt soon, Micah," she said, pushing him gently out the door while he still talked over his shoulder about the prospect of the reverend parting company with his skin.

When she returned from seeing him fairly to the garden gate, she sat down at the table and picked up the lame kitten, holding it on her lap under the cupped palm of her hand. The kitten reached up its ears and nose and tried to push through her fingers, shaking all over with its unpracticed purr. Puss stood this as long as possible, then hunched and leaped alongside. "There now," said Dorrie and made room for more cat by crooking her elbow. Puss snorted but settled.

They sat so, all four, in silence for a bit, then Dorrie stirred. "Reverend, would it be wrong in me to pray for Gideon?"

"It would be very right in you, child."

"I wouldn't ask for one thing or another, Reverend, I mean if he should stay or go. Likely he'll go, seeing there's his call, but I'd want to ask for him to be happy."

"We'll both pray."

"Should I pray to the Devil maybe?"

"No," said Birdsong sharply. "You may safely leave that with Mr. Lapp."

Dorrie shook her head. "Seems hard to believe Gideon'd be happy in those far-off places. He likes things as they should be, cow in pasture, bucket by the wellspring, pie in the oven maybe." She touched the kitten's nose, and Puss jealously batted her hand with his paw. "You know, Reverend?"

"What, Dorrie?"

"It's nice there's going to be another baby," said Dorrie.

# CHAPTER SEVEN

THE WOODLOT trees had no leaves on them and the air was cold enough so that the axe strokes sang silver. The white sky looked like early snow, and a rabbit rustled among the leaves, moving slower than it had in October.

Gideon split a thick branch and tossed it onto the pile growing beside him, taking pleasure from the bright chips and the sawdust smell that was wheaty and bitter at the same time.

He glanced up to figure where the sun would be if the clouds would let it, and it came to him that in a little while he would have to turn home if he wanted to work some more on the pen he was building before he went to milk the cow. The pen was for the pig, its journeying having become something of a scandal and its last appearance being made in Mr. Lunny's tavern. Mr. Lunny had taken the visit very unkindly and it had let him into a caterwauling with Sheby. Sheby had been sent pigging, and it was very true that Sheby's tongue, like the pig, was naturally born to trouble. She came home sobbing, having had the long way back to reflect on her manners and receiving no comfort whatever from the pig. The fine glory that had come from shouting at Mr. Lunny had curdled like milk in a thunderstorm by the time she saw her own chimney smoke. She was certain she had disgraced all the Briggses and she wept under the table while the whole family besought her to come out and be comforted. The drama had ended when Jabez crept in beside her with the warming news that Gideon would build the pig a home of its own and it would never wander more.

Gideon dropped a chunk of wood on his chopping block and thought mildly how all could have been made easier if the pig would sleep with the cow. The cow was willing enough, but the pig behaved so huffishly that the matter of sharing had to be given over completely. Gideon decided that, while he was building for the pig, he might as well be raising a coop for the two geese. This would astound them, but surely they would be pleased. They had been good geese and had lifted their webbed feet over much snow and mud without clamoring louder than usual, and they slept where they stood, sometimes in a tree fork, sometimes on the doorstep and sometimes, when they were so minded and nobody stopped them, at the bottom of Gramma's bed.

A coop for the geese, then, thought Gideon, and a pen for the pig. Comes the day we have three hens and a cock, they'll bed with the geese. He had a present dream of three hens and a cock and he did not know how he had come by that special number, but the cock stood clear in his mind as a weather vane. The hens would lay their eggs and do as the cock told them, but they would never be eaten.

Nothing that lived with the Briggs family ever got itself eaten. For all the many times the pig had been talked of as pork, not even the curl of its tail had stood in danger. The Briggs family would as soon have put Jabez in the stewpot, and the pig knew this very well. It was altogether a very cunning animal, and small wonder that Mr. Lunny thought ill of it. A cow who was still nervous in her feelings would surely be better off without the pig's company.

The little calf wouldn't be born before there was spring in the air and shelter not needed, and anyway Mr. Clegg would be wanting it back in his own barn as soon as it could do for itself. Cow would have to go back to Mr. Clegg too, once the tending was easy.

Gideon sighed and swung his axe, and the wood split so hard that half of it flew into the air. He picked it out of the brown leaves and tossed it on his pile, leaving the gathering for Obadiah and Shadrach. They were glad enough to do it, since an occasional woodmouse found its way in among the branches and they had heard that a woodmouse caught sleeping turns to gold.

The way to walk back home was through the cut and into his own yard, but Gideon went by the little field which he had tilled and harrowed and sowed and which had given its good yield and now lay brown and fallow. He leaned to take a handful of cold earth and ran it through his fingers, rich and very dark, with frost already deep in it and hidden, and hidden too the wild seeds that would thrust out green.

He forgot about time and crossed the whole length of the meadow, skirted its edge through thistle-heads and knotgrass and the woolly leaves of burdock and came finally to the fence that bounded Mr. Clegg's land. He put down his axe in a dry place and leaned on the top rail, staring over the roll of land toward the hem of dark trees that stood up straight and tall about Thomas Clegg's house. As he watched, the boy who tended for the old man and his wife came out of the barn carrying a milk pail and sauntered toward the house. He was a thin dangling child named Tattery and very clumsy with his hands so that Gideon suffered sometimes thinking about the cows, but Thomas Clegg's mean streak had widened with the years and Tattery worked for less than his keep.

There was talk in the village that Mr. Clegg had a room filled with gold to the roof, and the Reverend Lapp said that the old man was a friend to the Dark Neighbor himself, mentioning often how he would not give to the church, not even at high festivals. Gideon thought Mr. Clegg was only mean and dried up, dying a little at a time, but he wished with his whole heart that he had gold or silver or even stored up grain to offer him so that the visiting cow might stay with the Briggses forever, her and her little calf when it came.

He gave over thinking about it in a minute, but he stayed leaning on the fence and looking at the brown land lying asleep. A dry stalk of milkweed with its parchment seed pods brushed his hand, and he pulled off the big pod from the top and opened it slowly to satin lining and to the strange little silver-plumaged bird of seed tufts that was caged inside. He closed the pod up carefully and put it into his pocket for Sheby, who would dry the feather thing in the sun and store it up, against the day when a nest was needed for the slumber of the golden mouse. It was generally understood that a golden mouse was not a thing to be sold.

One silky feather clung to his finger and he blew it gently loose and watched it drift to the ground, wondering if there were such things as milkweed pods in the far-off places of India and Chiny. His father had never been much of a talker about the strange worlds he knew, only once in a while he would be standing looking out at the farm and there would suddenly be such a look in his eye that anyone could tell, whatever wonderful thing he might be seeing, it was not barren ground or springing grain or a field of flowers. Gideon could understand that. Sometimes in winter he would be staring himself at a twisted old apple tree, dark branches against dark sky, and a breath would pass over it and it would stand forth suddenly, May-sweet with blossoms as pink as an evening cloud. But he would not really be seeing it at all, any more than his father, standing in the home doorway, was really seeing great mournful castles or tall ships before the wind or marvelous temples carved from jewels.

A cold wind blew against Gideon and reminded him that the sun was dropping, and he picked up his axe and started home, reproaching himself for keeping the cow waiting with his fancies. When he reached the shed, even Micah was not around, which was surprising, and he went in to find the cow standing with bent head, chewing her cud and looking thoughtful.

"So," said Gideon, speaking softly, and he pulled up the milking-stool (which was not a milking-stool at all but had lived earlier by the hearthside) and looked inside the milk pail, making sure no spiders were crawling about, distracted by a thing with no corners in which to set up their webs.

The cow gazed at him passively over her shoulder as he settled beside her and, forehead pressed to warm flank, emptied her heavy bag, the pale milk foaming and spurting into the bright pail until it was full almost to the brim. She was coming down well now, Gideon thought with satisfaction, and he looked about him for the parcel of kittens that Micah had brought home from Dorrie's sheltering, intending to offer them their supper.

Not a kitten to be seen. It was very strange. No Micah, no

mewings and, now that he thought of it, a quiet outside the house that was not at all natural. He jumped up and pushed the stool out of the way and gave the cow's rump a grateful slap, starting toward the house with strides as long as the milk pail would allow without its slopping over.

Light shone through the window and his stepmother's shadow crossed it, looking so firm that Gideon shook his head at his fear and slowed his haste. When he opened the door, all was explained at once: outdoors silence, absent Micah, supperless kittens.

Dorrie was visiting and, as was only right and proper, everyone and everything was, in turn, visiting her.

There was Dorrie herself first, sitting very straight on the settle, something blue on her lap and her hair, which was the color of a hazelnut, tied back with a ribbon. She looked very pleasant, Dorrie did.

Then there was Ma, moving about the black stove and talking to the whole room about the way the stove behaved when it was crossed. There was Gramma, leaning back in her rocking-chair, old hands folded on her stomach, old feet rocking to the floor each time the chair came forward, rocking back, rocking forward again, chair squeaking a little. There was Obadiah and Shadrach, cross-legged on the floor; Micah on the table with his knees up to his chin, one shoe off and one of the missing kittens trying to fit into it; kitten in the woodbox, two kittens under the table; Sheby, standing, mid-floor, feet planted, thumb in mouth; Jabez, too old to creep but creeping anyway, in busy circles, last kitten following, patting his round bare heel with a furry paw.

Micah shouted, "Here's Gideon," and flew into the air, taking the startled kitten with him in its shoe.

Dorrie looked up shyly and said, "Good evening, Gideon," and then looked down again, smoothing the blue thing on her lap.

Ma turned from the stove and prodded Jabez with her toe. "Get offa the floor, baby. Crawl like a mole, you'll *be* a mole some day. Look, Gideon, what Dorrie's brought us. Quilt for the baby, so beautiful I'm scared to touch it."

Gideon put down the pail of milk and came across the floor to look at the quilt as Dorrie lifted it for him to see. It was as beautiful as Ma said, and a baby ought to sleep very happy under all that blueness with the tiny stitches and the curl of blue ribbon for its nose to joggle.

"See, Gideon, see," said Micah, circling Dorrie and Gideon and quilt. "Here's a rose. First thing baby'll see when it opens its eyes is this rose a-blooming. 'Twon't spit its milk, will it, ma, and spoil the rose? Will it?"

Gramma said, "Won't have no more teeth in its head than its granny. Why shouldn't it spit? Quilt's for using, ain't it? Ain't it, Dorrie?"

Dorrie said, "Oh, yes," bravely. Ma said firmly that the baby would always go under the quilt as neat and dry as a pea in its pod. Gideon was reminded of his gift for Sheby and he drew the milkweed pod out of his pocket, and Sheby drew her thumb out of her mouth.

"That's a fine one," Micah announced, dancing up and down and speaking for Sheby those things she did not say for herself. "All fine and soft."

Sheby looked at her brother much the way the geese looked at their beetles and, clutching her new treasure to her front, she slipped to a corner and unearthed a small blackened box from beneath a bed. Ma said, "Show it to Dorrie, the pretty box and all," and Sheby brought it over slowly, holding it out at cautious arm's length, little tin box with red lines on it that had once been patterned like frost.

"Oh, it's beautiful," said Dorrie, and Sheby came and leaned against her and opened the lid to show how it hinged, and inside was a double fistful of shiny seed-tufts, soft as angels.

"It's for if we ever catch a woodmouse sleeping," Sheby explained. "You know what happens if that happens, Dorrie?"

"It turns to gold," said Dorrie promptly.

"That's what it does," said Sheby, "and it will sleep on this nest, all gold and safe. Micah, take your fingers off!"

"It's soft," said Micah, ecstatic but obedient.

"Amos brought the box one time, Dorrie," said Martha, coming over to join them and touching the box lid. "Used always to bring us things when he came back but somehow that's past. He sells them off or barters them out, and nothing comes back in his pockets but a little dust. Well, we've got clutter enough. I think he *means* to bring us things," she added.

Sheby put the new pod in on top of the silky feathers and closed down the lid. "I'll sun it tomorrow," she said with satisfaction.

Dorrie got up and held out the quilt. "I'd best be going now," she said.

"It's the prettiest thing I ever saw, Dorrie," Martha said, holding a corner of blue up to her cheek. "All that work and the little stitches. You'll thank Miss Maidy, will you, for the ribbon?"

"She'll be happy," said Dorrie and gathered up her cloak.

Gideon said, "It's turned dark, I'll light you home," and lifted the lantern from its hook by the door. Dorrie said, "Oh, no," but he paid her no mind, only adding, "I've the milk to leave for Mr. Clegg, he gets half. Ma, where's the jug at?"

The milk was measured out, the quilt was praised again,

Micah collected the kittens for farewells, Gramma was nudged and nodded with eerie cordiality, being yet asleep. Dorrie and Gideon stepped over the doorsill and out into early night so black that nothing had shape except the wind which was stirring about the tree branches and lifting things to pry underneath. The geese went gabbling by, white blurs in the dark, and hissed when Gideon swung the lantern light over their sleek heads and gaping beaks.

"You've got the milk to carry, Gideon," Dorrie said after a moment. "Should I be taking the lantern to help you?"

"I've two hands," said Gideon. "Can you climb the stile in petticoats?"

"Oh, yes," Dorrie said.

"Then we'll not need to go around. It's farther by half." He held the lantern for her so that she walked on a dim-yellow circle of light with the stiff brown grass thrusting up sharp and patterned and all the hillocks shadowy to warn her stepping foot. The wind snatched at her cloak and tugged at her hair, and she pulled up her hood and felt wonderfully safe inside it, with the light to walk on and Gideon's shoulder so close. She should have started home earlier. Miss Maidy and Miss Emma might be worrying, the night so dark and no knowing how many boggles about, and Dorrie was a little troubled for them so that she walked as fast as she could though she would have liked to walk slow.

They came to the stile over Mr. Clegg's fence and Gideon held the lantern high. Dorrie went up lightly and down lightly, and Gideon carried the milk over without a drop spilled. There was only a thin glimmer of light from Mr. Clegg's house, a stingy crack against darkness, and Gideon knocked loud on the door. It creaked grudgingly, and Mrs. Clegg came out holding to it as if the wind might blow her over, which it might, she being sparrowy. She took the pail from Gideon's hand without saying anything and vanished, and a moment later she was back and handing it over empty.

"Thank you, ma'am," said Gideon.

She saw Dorrie suddenly, behind him, just as she was about to close the door and she leaned forward out into the night, still holding tight to the knob. "Good evening," she said, calling the two words though she was so close she could have whispered them.

Dorrie said, "Good evening, ma'am," and Mrs. Clegg gave her an anxious smile, wintry but sweet like a frosty apple. "It's cold tonight," said Mrs. Clegg. "I'll tell Thomas," and closed the door.

"It's lonely for her," said Dorrie, half aloud, and turned to follow the lantern. After quite a while, she said softly, "Gideon—"

"Dorrie?"

"It's not needful for you to take me all the way home, Gideon. I can find my own way now, we're that near the village."

Gideon said, "It was your kindness to bring the quilt," and she saw that he was returning favor with favor and said no more about it. It was true the night was very dark. There might be another storm in the making like the one on All Souls' Day, and it would be sad if she should stray into the river and drown, causing everybody much concern and anxiety.

When they left the growing-ground and came onto the hard road that led into the village, Dorrie ventured thanks to Gideon for taking the five kittens.

"It was Micah's doing, not mine," said Gideon. "He said you

kept the one that was lame."

"It needed teaching," said Dorrie apologetically.

"Teaching, Dorrie?"

"To learn to do on the three legs," said Dorrie. "Like a milking stool. Gideon, is it true you're not to keep the cow or the calf?"

"It's true as you heard it," said Gideon, a little roughly.

"I'm sorry."

"It was agreed on."

"But I'm sorry anyway," said Dorrie, more firmly than she was used to speaking. "You ought to be having either the cow herself or the calf when it comes."

He was silent for so long a while that Dorrie thought he was angry, and under her sheltering cloak she felt a little frightened. Gideon said, finally, "Ma's always told me she makes bread from the flour that's to hand, Dorrie. Mr. Clegg is not a giving man."

"I'm sorry," said Dorrie, very small. "It wasn't for me to talk about."

Gideon said, as if he had not heard the small voice, "It's against my wishing. I'd be glad with my whole heart to leave them a cow when I go. Things will be hard enough then without the cow's being gone."

"Oh, Gideon," Dorrie burst out, unable to stop herself, "must you go, can't you stay?"

"I'll go when my call comes," Gideon said patiently.

"It's wicked," said Dorrie. "I know it's wicked. You should not listen to it, it's wrong to be listening."

He flung his hand out sharply, and the lantern light swung away from guiding her feet. "Do you think I want to go?" he demanded. "Do you think I'd not stay forever if I could? It's no more of my choosing than the sun going down. Dorrie—"

She caught her breath at the pain in his voice. He said suddenly, "We'll not talk of it," and the lantern's circle came back to light the path.

Neither of them spoke again until they passed the tavern, when Mr. Lunny's queer little dog ran out barking, saw that he knew who they were and ran in again, his duties attended. "Oh, it's late," Dorrie cried. "Mr. Lunny's lit his evening fire or the dog would not be in. I'll hurry, Gideon, I must. Supper's not laid and Puss not fed, and you must be home to your own supper. I can see my way now by the street and it's only to the next turn—Gideon?"

He held the lantern up and looked at her. "What is it, Dorrie?"

"You're not angry with me?" she said timidly.

He said with wonder, "Why would I be angry? You've done nothing but good. Good night then, Dorrie." He turned and left her, and she stood still for so long a moment that it was a wonder the little dog didn't hear her silence and come out to sniff at it.

When she remembered how late she was, she turned about and picked up her skirts and ran, causing one or two to stare at her but arriving on her doorstep just in time to find Miss Maidy getting into a bonnet to go out and find her.

"Blessed be!" said Miss Maidy, giving a cry of joy and taking off her bonnet at once so the roses on it would not be shaken by her relief. "We thought you'd gone wandering and lost yourself, nothing's safe in November and Puss in a maze about something."

"I'm sorry," said Dorrie penitently, throwing back her hood and unfastening her cloak.

"There, it's no matter," Miss Maidy said comfortably, unable to hold to her grievance for even a moment. "Nothing's to rights though, and Sister can't even find the hen-cozy for the teapot. I do wish Mrs. Lapp would be more agreeable about the hen-cozy, Dorrie, though she's very Christian in most things. Sister's in the kitchen. She gave your lame kitten some cream which I thought wasteful, but wasn't it kind? Do lay supper quickly, dear, you know how Emma is about keeping hours. Only run and tidy your hair first. You look," said Miss Maidy unexpectedly, "so pretty."

Dorrie stared at her blankly, then turned and sped up the narrow flight to her attic room where she laid aside her cloak and stepped quick to the mirror, meaning only to smooth her hair and retie the ribbon before she went down.

She took the ribbon off and shook her hair loose, and it fell all around her shoulders in a soft veil. She looked at her face but she could not see what Miss Maidy meant at all, it being too broad to be pretty and her eyes not blue and wonderful like Sheby's but only plain gray. It was a face that served for the week and went nicely enough to church on Sundays, and if it looked pretty to Miss Maidy it must have been because she was so glad to see it come back.

Dorrie leaned a little closer to the mirror. Her cheeks were pink from the high wind, and her hair was shiny. Maybe her hair could be called pretty, though it was tumbled about. She stared at herself looking back at herself for quite a long moment, and then she spoke to the Dorrie in the mirror.

"I'd like for Gideon to see my hair so," said Dorrie. She put the backs of her hands to her cheeks and felt them hot.

Then she stopped looking at the foolish girl in the mirror and braided her hair up very tight and ran out of the room as fast as her feet would carry her. She had Puss to care for, and the lame kitten. She had Miss Emma to be seeing to, and Miss Maidy, and the hen-cozy that would not be found.

# CHAPTER EIGHT

SNOW CAME from the north.

It fell all night long without stir, easy as a sigh. The ruts in the road filled till the road was all level, running between snow-roofed houses with doorsteps rounded like bread loaves. The brown leafed, dry-stalked gardens vanished. Snow capped the fence posts, and each branch of the big elm tree that sheltered the church was black stroke under white.

The snow sifted through the willows that leaned over the Meander and fell into its dark stream, water touching water. In the deep woods, it was all heavy hush except one moment when a great-winged owl swooped and a tiny explosion of mouse-tracks scuttled to tree roots. The old badger grunted in his sleep, and a rooster, roused by so much whiteness, started to crow and thought better of it.

Martha Briggs woke at dawn and went barefoot to the door, standing there with arms akimbo, shivering and looking out until she scolded herself for trying to catch a death of cold and turned back into the house. She covered Gramma up a bit warmer and Gramma in her sleep said "Girl" as if she knew where special kindnesses came from.

In the shed that Gideon had built, the five kittens curled in hay, and the geese, who had wandered in at first sign of goose feathers falling from the sky, nested down at a haughty distance. The cow, hospitable whether she wished or not, tasted snow on her tongue and thought no more about it. The pig slept and made noises like a stew kettle, and if it dreamed of anything it dreamed of slops and trouble.

In the village, the Reverend Lapp woke in his narrow bed and saw the great soft flakes pressing against the windowpane. A sense of duty warring with the downy warmth of sleep caused him to clamber out in his nightshirt and go to the window where his Sunday sermon lay spread before him—the sinning earth beneath the purity of the snow. He would work out the moral later. The sound of his mother stirring about in the kitchen below caused him to reflect moodily on recent lumps in the porridge, and he began to dress with a text from *Lamentations*.

The Reverend Birdsong, waking at about the same time, discovered a large cat named Charity sitting on his feet and a pile of snow on the windowsill beyond. The morning was beautiful without, and cozy within. "God's blessings are eternal," said Birdsong drowsily and put his nose back in his pillow from which there shortly rose a clerical snore. Charity blinked green eyes and settled down, purring her music.

Dorrie, up before the sun, ran out to see the snow-hedged garden and got her feet wet, so she had to take off her shoes and set them at the stove, this side of Puss and other side of the lame kitten. Puss ignored the dawn, but the kitten sat up dutifully to wash its face. This done, it hunched over its saucer of milk and dipped its whiskers so deep that all the washing was to do again. Distracted by the turn of events, it went and leaned against

Puss. Puss woke and spat, turned around grumbling and let the vagrant settle against his furry haunches.

Dorrie got out pail and scrub brush and pumped water at the sink. She had meant to set a sponge for bread-raising first, but having bare feet it seemed a good time to scrub the floor. She rolled her sleeves firm and high above her elbows and tucked her skirt about her knees.

Cats sleeping, water sloshing, white world outside and warm world in, Dorrie scrubbed. It was nice about the snow, she thought, December being so forward already. Green Christmas was a full churchyard, and now the small cemetery could sleep quiet, though there was word about the village that Mr. Clegg had been taken bad again. Perhaps he would die and leave the cow to Gideon. . . .

Dorrie sat back on her heels and made a hasty cross in the air against the Evil Eye and for the favor of God, because it was wrong even to think of Mr. Clegg dying when he, poor old man, probably had no wish to. She thought instead about the coming season of the Lord's birthday, with the sweet cakes and the hot mince and the lemony-grog that Miss Emma was so fond of. There would be much baking and bustle and old tunes and, in some houses, though not in this one, kissing-boughs hung over doorways. There would be bright cold stars and the church bells and the candle-walking at Christmas midnight when all the villagers came, each with his own lit candle, walking through the street to the open church door.

Most candles blew out, and that meant those who carried them would not be given their year's wish, but one or two stayed as steady as if the flame could not feel any wind, and those would be blessed. Dorrie's candle had gone out last year, snuffed early, and she had lost her wish but, to tell the truth, it had been such a small domestic one it was not much to be missing.

This year she knew already what her wish was to be. She would wish that Gideon's call would never come, and she would carry her candle so shielded and so safe behind her fingers that the flame would burn like a star.

A thump of snow shook itself loose from above the door and landed amidst Miss Emma's herb bed, waking Dorrie out of Christmas. She jumped up and stood for a moment, running wet hands over her skirt and leaving patches like a frogpond, then fled to her shoes which were not dry and very averse to being put on.

Outside the window, snow slid again from the roof and landed softly on winterbound balm and tansy, on sweet basil and marjoram and thyme.

By midday, it was sliding from eaves all about Greenwillow as the sun touched it loose, and there were crusty places where it melted to the sun and froze to the wind.

Micah, fox tracking across the meadow, found such a glistering place and gave a shout as he leaped on it, cracking the bright glaze into stars and splinters. It was deeper than he had expected and he came up thoughtful, like a wet muskrat, but the pleasant thrown-about look he had now given the snow-filled meadow put him in mind of the pig. It would not, he thought, be amiss to go around by Mr. Clegg's and borrow a few ears of corn from the near-bursting corncrib. He had to borrow them secretly both for his own sake and Mr. Clegg's, because if he asked for them straight Mr. Clegg would say no and there would be trouble all round. Micah did not believe in trouble.

He stomped his way through the rest of the meadow, having already unsmoothed it so, and, quiet and quick as the red fox he had been after, he slipped through the fence, down the gully and past the old well where Mr. Proudfoot had seen the Devil. The well was dry, years away, because a boggle had once dropped into the bottom of it and gulped it empty to get out. The boggle made off, but the water never came back.

Micah stopped to look into the well, just in case, but there was nothing inside and he was not really sad about it because he had expected nothing. He was about to enter the farmyard and scuttle to the corncrib when he saw the boy Tattery come out of the barn and start toward the house.

Corn ears forgotten, Micah hailed him and bounded through the snow to meeting. Tattery was cautious and lived like he was inside a hollow log, but Micah thought this might have something to do with his nose always being so blue in winter. It was true enough that, in the humming bee-days of June, Tattery's nose was quite natural and he had even been heard to sing through it. Just now it was blue again and best company for an icicle, but Micah, having circled him once to see if anything was new, said sociably, "I near caught a fox."

This was not quite correct. What he had near caught was some paw marks, and these he had lost when he leaped on the glistering place. Tattery, however, looked respectful, which was all that Micah wished.

Micah said, " 'Twere a big one with a brush like a flaming tree and great gold eyes a-glittering." This picture convinced him so that he was also able to recall a forked tongue. "Likely the Devil in fox's shape," said Micah, inspired.

Tattery shook his head soberly. "Devil's up with Mister Clegg," he said.

Micah gave an unselfish cry of astonishment.

"He's dying again," said Tattery.

"Mister Clegg is a-dying?" said Micah. "Devil's come for Mister Clegg?"

Tattery nodded. "The reverends have come too," he said. "Mis' Clegg, she sent me to the village to get Reverend Birdsong because Mister Clegg felt so bad. Reverend Lapp, he come by and heard all what I was telling and said he was coming too. He said the Devil was after Mister Clegg's soul and Reverend Birdsong didn't know ways to wrestle with the Devil."

"Sweet gracious!" said Micah. "They're a-wrestling now?"

"Reverend Lapp, he's wrestling. Reverend Birdsong, he just sits by the bed. Mister Clegg, he lies flat on his back and glares at 'em both."

"Devil peeps through his eyeballs likely," said Micah with hopefulness. "Tattery, I've never rightly seen the Devil. C'n I look through the window?"

Tattery considered this. He was seldom in a position to give anyone anything, and it warmed him inside like ginger root so that he lingered the moment, tasting it. "Could likely be done," he said cautiously, and Micah shouted with triumph.

Together they broke new snow and trailed to the window which Tattery pointed out. The sill was high and Micah clutched and slipped before he could hang on its edge and peer into the room.

First he saw the Reverend Lapp, very tall at the foot of the bed, with his arms wide like a crow's wings and his mouth busy with talking. Then he saw the Reverend Birdsong, sitting on a chair with his hands folded and his head on one side, giving an occasional nod now and then. And last he saw Mr. Clegg propped up on his pillows. His eyes were closed so the Devil, having no peepholes, might have come out into the room, but, though Micah squirmed and craned, not a sign of the Evil One was to be seen.

Mr. Birdsong glanced up through the window, and Micah let go hastily and fell off into the snow where he sat with his legs sticking out and a feeling that the Devil had outdone him. Tattery, taller by two inches, took his place and announced, "Devil's gone, Micah. No use us hunting."

"How do you know?" said Micah, rising and shaking himself.

"Mister Clegg ain't dying any more, sleeping natural he is. Reverends is leaving." He looked regretful. "Happens all the time, Micah. 'Tisn't really my fault."

"No," said Micah, being fair-minded, and skipped around to the front of the house to get behind a heath bush just as the two ministers came out the door, with Mrs. Clegg fretting behind them.

"I'm that sorry to have called you out," said Mrs. Clegg worriedly, "but he seemed so bad, and I'm fearful for him to die without the consolations."

"We must be on guard against the Evil One at all times," the Reverend Lapp observed, rather coldly. He was still smarting from Thomas Clegg's reception of those who came to save his soul. Rigid under the bedclothes, he had greeted his visitors with a snarl and glared at them out of filmy eyes. It was spite, thought the Reverend Lapp wearily, that had rallied the old man, pushing the Devil off his chest. Birdsong had been no help, sitting like a stove-pot and remarking at intervals that Mr. Clegg might rather be alone.

Lapp shook himself and, nodding from a height to Mrs. Clegg, stalked off through the snow, with his colleague only too pleased to follow in his large and sheltering footsteps.

Mrs. Clegg, sighing and shaking her head, went back into the house. Micah abstracted himself from the heath bush and went to tell Tattery that the Devil had been routed. "Allus around," said Tattery, not impressed. "He'll be back."

Micah leaped into the sky, came down facing the other way and, having little more to say to Tattery and much to tell his own family, set off at a wild flounder through the snow. Tattery shrugged and scrubbed his blue nose with the back of his hand, used to a life of comings and goings.

Micah whooped through the meadow, jumped the brush pile and spared scarcely a glance for the cowshed, hurtling into the house as if he rode a comet. Gramma and Ma and Sheby being all that was about, he took them for his audience and, waving his arms to the danger of the air, he announced with pride that he had near glimpsed the Devil.

Sheby, cross-legged on the floor and rocking in crooked arms the baby that would be born in June, glanced up at him, glanced down and continued to hum maternally. This outraged Micah, as it was intended to do, and he said rashly that he had seen the Devil, he had indeed, and it had come out of old Mr. Clegg's mouth on a puff of smoke.

Ma said, "Where's my stirring spoon?" but Gramma sat up and took an interest. "Thomas Clegg, eh?" said Gramma. "What was he doin' with the Devil in his mouth?"

"He was a-dyin'," said Micah solemnly.

Even Sheby stopped her exasperating lullaby. Ma said, "Micah! Mister Clegg's not dead, is he?"

Micah said no, Mr. Clegg was not dead. The Devil had come out into the room and the Reverend Lapp had thrown him to the floor and wrestled with him for nigh on two hours, tail thrashing about like a bright fish, Devil's tail, that was.

Ma said mildly, "How come you saw all this?"

"Hangin' from the windowsill," said Micah candidly.

"For two hours. That was nice. Now tell us what really happened."

"Mister Clegg, he almost died," said Micah, unruffled. "Reverends came and prayed for his soul, and Mister Lapp, he said the Devil was striving with them. But then Mister Clegg he falls nice asleep and isn't going to die after all. I wish he would die," said Micah pleasantly. "Then we could keep the cow."

A look of real longing came into Ma's eyes for a second, but she shook her head at Micah. "You shouldn't ever wish for a thing like that, lovey," she said, "and anyway 'twouldn't work out that way. Mister Clegg'd have to say special he was leaving us the cow, otherwise it goes right back in his barn when the calf comes, same as Gideon promised. Makes no difference, dead or alive."

"That ain't right," said Gramma suddenly.

"It's how it is."

"Well, it ain't right," said Gramma, giving the rocking chair such a hitch that it walked six inches. "Gideon's a good boy and it ain't right for him to be scrapin' and scroungin' to keep a cow what's goin' to go right back to that old misery. It ain't—" She gave a sudden delighted yelp. "Courted me once, he did. I ever tell you that, girl?"

"Who courted you, Gramma?"

"That old misery Clegg," said Gramma, giving a frivolous cackle. "Like to break his heart, he did, when I wed y'r grampa, threatened to drown hisself in the Meander. Not much water in it that summer, there wasn't, but enough to drown a skinny like Thomas." She sighed heavily. "I was real good to look at, back then. The men was like bees around a honeysuckle. Had trouble keepin' my virtue, I did." She looked around for her granddaughter and said sharply, "Sheby, mind that, time comes for you. I got me a good man, I did, all because I kept my virtue. At least, I think I kept it," said Gramma. "It's a long ways back."

Martha said, "You and Mister Clegg really walked out together?"

Gramma began to rock. "He wasn't so bad, I'll have you know," she said. "Ain't kept hisself like I have, but then he didn't start so good neither. He ain't got my gums. Married a poor spindly wife and didn't raise no children, set hisself to miserin' instead. My man never made no gold but look it the young uns I've got around me now. All yours, ain't they, girl?"

"All but Gideon."

"Gideon had a different ma," said Gramma, getting sleepy. "Micah, where's my turnip at?"

Micah who had found a kitten on the table put it in her lap. Gramma stroked its back straight down from round head to furry tip. "Can't chew a kitten's tail," she said and brushed it onto the floor, where it rolled over and played a wild game with the chair rockers. Micah went and got a new turnip out of the wooden bin and, bringing it, laid his head against Gramma's bony shoulder.

"Seems like it ought to be our cow if Mister Clegg dies," he said.

"Courted me, he did," said Gramma, nodding with sleep and clutching the turnip like treasure. "Could still give him a piece of my mind, if I'd a wish to."

Micah's toes curled inside his shoes. "He don't need three

cows," said Micah.

"When he's dead," said Gramma, "he won't even need one. Ain't never heard any stories that the Devil likes milk." She yawned and nearly lost her chaw of turnip. "Girl! You think I should wear my meeting-dress, the one I wear to church in oncet?"

Martha turned, puzzled. "What you want your meeting-dress for, ma?"

"F'r calling on Thomas Clegg, that's what I want it f'r." Her eyes closed, the turnip rolled from her hands, and the kitten followed it to the corner of the room. "Courted me once, he did," said Gramma slowly. "Wild rose time, and right on through the haying. I think I'd ought to wear my meeting-dress, it'd be better." Her words fell off and rolled away like the turnip, and her chin found itself a place on her front to settle.

"Sure, your meeting-dress," said Martha, coming over and staying to look down at her gently. Old dreams following themselves about in old heads, all raveled and twisted. Hope I have 'em too when I'm that old, thought Martha and went back to the stove, forgetting Thomas Clegg.

Even Micah forgot him, the old man asleep on his bed and the Devil gone out with the reverends. Nothing more to think about there, and Sheby to vex and so handy. Only Gramma remembered, even in sleep. The old man and the young lovers, and Gideon who ought to have the cow, and the meeting-dress that had been to church, all of them turned over and over in her dreams. She stirred once and spoke up real sharply, telling Thomas Clegg what he was to do about the cow.

# CHAPTER NINE

**M**RS. LAPP, coming down the street, averted her eyes from the tavern door just in time to see the Reverend Birdsong go through it. She had been progressing in a spirit of Christian charity with a bowl of arrowroot for Meg Chessy, the carpenter's wife, who was poorly, but the spectacle of the clergyman entering the tavern stopped her short. Mrs. Lapp hoped she knew a higher duty when she saw one.

She took a stronger grip on Meg Chessy's arrowroot and planted her feet firmly, intending to wait for Mr. Birdsong and present him with a piece of her mind. But the wind blew cold after a very short interval, and she had worn her second-best cloak, it being only Meg Chessy, and it did not seem needful that she should be carried off with a chill on Mr. Birdsong's behalf. Discoursing to herself on the prevalence of Mr. Birdsong's sins, she marched off on her errand of mercy, bowing grimly to Miss Maidy who was patting by with a basket on her arm.

Later she regretted this, as Miss Maidy should have been told about the clergyman's iniquities. Still, there was always Meg and poor Meg would be very glad to have village news, bedridden as she was and with a husband who seldom said more than a grunt.

The Reverend Birdsong, unaware that he had been causing anguish to Mrs. Lapp, sat placidly by the tavern fireside and watched while Mr. Lunny transferred a potation of golden brandy, drop by drop, from a large bottle to the small one his visitor had brought. The brick hearth was occupied by Little Fox Jones and Mr. Lunny's black and white dog, and the Reverend Birdsong sang to them both, though they were asleep. It was a small garland song, all about the field flowers that bloomed in the hay where the baby Jesus slept, and there was a pleasant refrain which the Reverend Birdsong tapped out with his foot:

> Sing to Mary, sing to Joseph
> The flowers opened where He lay.

After a while, Mr. Lunny, who was not as quick in his head as he was in his fingers, learned the refrain and joined in, and they made a small festivity of the song and fireside with the snow outside for the blessed season and the sun sparkling through the window glass.

"There," said Mr. Lunny, holding the little bottle to the light where it looked like a honey-bee. "Fifty-two drops exactly, one for each week of the year. It would be for the brandy-pudding, I take it, Reverend?"

"The brandy-pudding, yes," said Mr. Birdsong, nodding. "Mrs. Likewise puts citron and lemon peel and ginger and a handful of currants into it, and the whole thing is boiled in a bag, producing an object of extraordinary merit and great durability."

"You mean it keeps well," said Mr. Lunny.

"It keeps very well," said Mr. Birdsong with conviction. "I have even found bits of it around on Midsummer Eve, defying reason." He put the little bottle into his pocket, said a courteous goodbye to Little Fox Jones and the black and white dog, still sleeping, and bowed gravely to Mr. Lunny.

"You'll be preaching for the candle-walking, Reverend?" said Mr. Lunny.

"Well, no, Mr. Lapp will. I believe he wants to speak out against the candle-walkers." He sighed. "It is selfish perhaps to ask for ourselves on the night of the Birth when our hearts should be especially humble, but I have never been able to make up my mind that He would object."

"It don't matter Mr. Lapp's preaching against it, once we've got our wishes made," said Mr. Lunny charitably. "I got my wish one year, before you came, Reverend, my little dog so sick he'd like to die. I wished him to be well with my old heart in the wishing, and my candle stayed lit right up to the altar and through all the preaching, and past moontime and into the sun coming up. I walked down the street with the dawn, and there was my little dog waiting for me. His tail was fine and high and his eyes were as bright as two haw berries." He cast an affectionate glance at the dozing object of his pride and included Little Fox Jones from force of habit. " 'Twas nice, wasn't it?"

The Reverend Birdsong nodded thoughtfully, quite understanding why the Reverend Lapp was so determined to preach the candle-walking.

"Told Mr. Lapp about it, I did," said Mr. Lunny, answering Mr. Birdsong's thoughts, "and he said I was blaspheming. But, then, he don't have a dog." He pinched his lower lip between thumb and forefinger and scowled. "Likely I should have wished for something else, but the candle-walking wish is the one that always comes about and, to be true with you, Reverend, I could not bear for my little dog to die."

"No," said the Reverend Birdsong.

"Well, God bless us all," said Mr. Lunny. "This year I shall wish for a upstanding chimney. Nothing in that to vex Mr. Lapp's heart, and it does seem sometimes that the wind has a grudge against me."

"In that case," said Mr. Birdsong comfortably, "it will come over your shoulder and blow your candle out."

Mr. Lunny guffawed, and his dog and Little Fox Jones twitched in their sleep. The Reverend Birdsong accepted Mrs. Likewise's brandy and went out the door with a light step and a cheerful countenance.

There was a cross of whitethorn or a sprig of holly or a spray of sweet-smelling fir over every doorway, with Christmas Day just around the bend of the week. The littlest children in the village had gone greening with the biggest ones, venturing very far out into woods so old that souls still lived in the trees; and they brought back tangles of wintergreen and loops of ground pine with the snow wet and heavy on them. These they hung, singing, above the church door, and inside they garlanded the altar with ivy, which was believed to attract the blessed saints and not allowed indoors at any other season of the year.

Aggie Likewise boiled her pudding in its bag and put it on the top shelf in the pantry, next to a pomander ball. It gave out such an exhilarating fragrance that the cats went about at a trot instead of a stroll, and the Reverend Birdsong found numerous things of importance to do in its vicinity.

Even Mrs. Lapp got out her hoard of thick dark sugar and sprinkled it on her son's porridge for three days before

Christmas, although she knew it would endanger his digestion and make spirituality more difficult. In almost every house but theirs, there was much sorting of candles for the candle-walking and long leisurely arguments among neighbors as to whether a fat or a thin candle would stand the wind best. There were some who scooped a hole out about the flame to make a safe place for it, but if it was not to stay alight it would not. By the time the church had been circled, as it must be, there would be few candles left burning. This was so even on the stillest night, and it was why so few wishes came true and why the candle-walking was such a wonderful mysterious thing.

By high sun time on the day before Christmas, Dorrie had chosen her candle, not because it was fat or thin but because it was as white as a christening robe and as straight as the church steeple. She would not breathe as she carried it, not until she was safe inside the church itself with the flame still burning, and then she would let her breath go and give thanks that her wish was safe and Gideon would never get his call.

Once her candle was chosen, she put it out of her mind because it was so worrying. Besides she was busy between stove and table, making gingerbread fancies with a sugar and water paste to decorate them, stars put on with the back of a spoon and little wheels and crescents and angel wings, all colored in yellow with last summer's meadow saffron. The warm ginger smell was lovely, and Miss Emma kept coming into the kitchen to ask Dorrie's opinion on her church bonnet which had a white plume for Christmas Day. Each time she departed, she took a gingerbread fancy with her, and Miss Maidy pattered behind to warn her about her digestion. As Miss Maidy also bore off her own gingerbread fancies, the little cakes had a certain cloudlike quality of vanishing.

Dorrie had just coaxed another twelve off their hot pan and set them to cool when there was a tap at the door, about so loud as a woodmouse might make. The lame kitten went to see who was there, being hospitable, but the doorknob was beyond kitten reach and Dorrie had to help, opening it wide to find Micah on the step with Jabez clutching raggletail to his coat.

"Blessed be your Christmas, Dorrie," said Micah, gabbling the correct greeting for the day. "We'd not want to be troubling you, but with the midnight so near and all—" He broke off, his nose twitching at the spicy kitchen smell.

"Umm," said Jabez, like velvet.

"Come in, then," said Dorrie resignedly and got out of their way, she and the kitten, just in time. Micah and Jabez were most polite however and, when Jabez stuffed two gingerbread fancies into his pocket, Micah rapidly explained that they were for feeding the birds on the way home.

"Poor little feathers and all," said Micah with mute sentiment, "you'd not have them forgotten at the Lord's feast, would you?"

Jabez looked at him anxiously but said nothing. He was not unmannerly to birds, but on every bush there were plenty of berries still about and many seeds clinging to all the stalky things that grew in the meadow, not to mention pine cones and winter grasses and bits of corn that the pig was careless with. Birds must be so full that gingerbread fancies would be bad for them, even. He decided to explain this to Micah after they left and, satisfied, he sat down with the brindled cat.

"What brings you?" said Dorrie, looking into the oven and shaking her head at the kitten who was tangling about her feet. Then she said suddenly, "Gideon's not had his call, Micah?" with her heart in her mouth.

"Not that," said Micah. "It's our having a cow on Christ
midnight." He sat down on the floor and pulled his knees u
his chin like a goblin on its hob. "Gideon says, and he kn
such things, that on the night of the Birth, just when the b
are ringing in all the churches—they's churches all over
world, not just ours here, did you know that, Dorrie?"

Yes, said Dorrie, she knew that.

"Some time I must go to church," said Micah serene
"there's so much doing."

"Tell about the cow," said Jabez crossly.

"Surely, the cow," Micah agreed. "Gideon says that, whe
the midnight bells start a-ringing all over the wide earth, i
comes into the minds of the cows and the sheep and the big
bulls, even the traveling bull hisself, it comes into their minds to
kneel down in the straw. And do you know for why, Dorrie?"

"To do honor to the Christ child," said Dorrie. "It's quite
true, Micah, what Gideon told you."

Micah, prepared for astonishment, was somewhat cast
down, but then it came to him how splendid it was that both
Gideon and Dorrie knew this noble thing to be true, and he
could see at once that it was now twice as true so that possibly
even the pig might kneel.

He licked the saffrony sugar off a fancy, curling his tongue
and his toes in contentment, took a large bite and said, with his
mouth full, "So, will you come, Dorrie?"

"Come where, Micah?" said Dorrie, startled.

"To watch the cow kneel at midnight, of course."

"Oh," Dorrie said and put her hand to her heart to hide the
eagerness of its beating. "Did Gideon ask you to tell me,
Micah?"

"Certain," said Micah.

"Oh, I would like it," Dorrie breathed, and then she gave a little cry that was nearly a moan. "Micah, I can't. There's the candle-walking, I couldn't miss that. I've a special wish this year."

Micah gave a grieved cluck. "We'd forgot that," he said mournfully. "Comes of not being churchly folk, does it not, Dorrie? Is it a good wish, Dorrie, the one you've got?"

"It's very important." She longed to tell him what it was, but there was danger of something overhearing her and being vexed by an early telling, so she closed her lips against sharing.

"You mustn't tell, of course," said Micah wisely, then rose suddenly, bowing, as Miss Emma came into the kitchen again, still perplexed by her bonnet. "Blessed be your Christmas, ma'am," said Micah.

"Blessed be yours, child," said Miss Emma cordially. "What's that under the table?"

"Jabez," said Jabez, who knew.

"How nice," Miss Emma agreed. She held her bonnet up in her hand and twirled it briskly about so they could see all sides of it. Dorrie sighed gently in admiration.

"You'll be wearing that to church tonight?" said Micah, examining the bonnet by walking around it. "I wish I could be there to see it a-bobbing along, but I'll be with the cow come midnight."

"It will kneel down, you know," said Miss Emma.

Micah gave an outraged exclamation. "How comes it everyone knows this but me?" he demanded. "I could have found cows other Christmases, and been a-watching and a-helping them. Why does no one tell me until now?"

"You never had a cow before, Micah," Dorrie said, "and maybe other cows, not knowing you, wouldn't kneel when you

were there."

"Suppose ours won't?" said Micah.

"Oh, Micah!"

Dorrie looked so distressed that Micah's disappointment fled him completely, and he said, "There, Dorrie, don't be worrying. Cow will kneel all right, and likely the pig will kneel too."

"Pigs don't kneel," said Miss Maidy, coming into the kitchen and flapping her white apron at Micah and Jabez as if they had been chickens in her garden. "They fall over sideways sometimes with their feet sticking out."

"Blessed be your Christmas, ma'am," said Micah. "That's true, they do fall over."

"Emma dear, I hope you're not eating ginger— Oh, your bonnet's ready! How lovely. Children, do get along, do. Dorrie's so busy, and Christmas tomorrow. Isn't Miss Emma's bonnet lovely?"

Jabez came forth suddenly, wailing, and said that the cat had eaten his gingerbread fancy. Micah set his brother's round cap straight on his head, smacked his rear absent-mindedly and pushed him toward the door. "I'll be by again," he said hospitably, "and tell you about the cow kneeling. Walk happy with your candle, Dorrie. I hope it'll not blow out."

Dorrie kneeled suddenly and embraced them both, surprising Jabez almost beyond belief, not because he lacked for loving at home but because it was not true about the cat eating his fancy and he knew that Dorrie knew. Confused but happy, he let himself be led away by Micah, who spun him an unusual account of the Lord's birth all the way home and even took him past the boggle's well. Later there would be the cow's kneeling, and Jabez felt he could scarcely wait.

But when the time came before midnight, the sky full of stars and one star in particular, not only Jabez had to be wakened from his corner but Micah and Sheby and Obadiah and Shadrach as well. Gideon shook them each by the shoulder and they stared up at him, furry with sleep, before they could remember the cow and the hour of the night and what night it was.

Gideon took the lantern down and lit it while they yawned themselves awake and then, moving softly with Rip following behind on quiet pads, they stepped out into the snow and all the stars.

The pig in its lean-to scarcely stirred, unmindful of the blessed night. Sheby, who felt responsible for its odd customs, said it was not really sleeping at all but saying its prayers with its eyes closed. No one believed this of the pig except Obadiah who was impressionable and given to asking questions about the Holy Bible, which for some reason he supposed to be a river.

Gideon pushed the shed door open while Micah held the lantern high, and the cow turned her head and looked at them from a circle of light. The warm smell of hay and the rich cow-smell hung heavy on the air, cold enough and yet not cold at all. Sheby went to put her arms around the cow's neck. "Blessed be your Christmas," said Sheby, stepping back, and the cow looked at her with liquid eyes and blew out breath in a little puff of frosty air.

Jabez sat down in the straw and a goose came over and pecked him. Sheby said it was Jabez's own fault, and Jabez tried to cajole Rip into biting the goose's tail. Gideon said passively for them all to be quiet, midnight was almost on them, and they folded their hands and caught their breaths and listened for time to pass.

"How will we know?" said Micah, very soft so as not to disturb midnight or the cow.

"By the bell from the church," said Gideon.

"It will ring and the cow will kneel?" said Micah.

"That's how it will be," said Gideon.

Micah was still for a whole moment. "That's when the Baby Jesus gets born," he said, turning his head to explain to everybody. "He gets born, and the cow kneels, all the cows kneel. All over the world, Gideon?"

Gideon nodded.

"Where Pa is too?" said Micah.

"I suppose so, Micah."

"Where's midnight?" said Micah, not prone to wait.

"When the bell rings," Gideon said, apparently not vexed by the question. He was staring at the cow, its curly horns and its filled-out white flanks and its calm way of chewing. He felt a great softness for it and for the calf it was sheltering and even for the traveling-bull that had made the calf. He wondered if what he had told Micah was true, that the cattle kneeled all over the world on the Holy night, and he wondered too where Pa was.

"Gideon," said Micah, whispering loud and tugging at Gideon's sleeve. "Midnight almost. Dorrie will be walking to the church with her candle lit and her wish to make. What do you suppose her wish might be, Gideon?"

"A good one, whatever it is," said Gideon, and he had a sudden vision of Dorrie, her cloak about her shoulders and her hood shielding her face and hair, the stars bright over her head and the candle light steady as a star itself between her fingers. The softness within him spread, and he remembered how kind she had been with the quilt for the baby. It would be nice, he thought, if she could have been beside him now, watching the cow and waiting to hear the bell.

"Gideon," said Micah restlessly.

"Hush," said Gideon, "and listen."

The air stirred, the Star shone, and up from the village there came the first clear note of the midnight bell. The cow turned her head away from her watchers, listening, and they held their breaths, waiting for all the animals in all the stables of the world to kneel because the Saviour was being born. Sheby thought what a tiny baby He must have been, and she hugged her arms against her breast, cradling Him since in this small stable He was here but His Mother was not.

"Cow's not kneeling," said Micah, alarmed.

"The bell is still ringing, Micah," Gideon told him. "Don't be fearful. The cow will kneel."

The bell was in full call now, and an echo of it came back from out of frost and cold and black midnight, so that it stayed hung on the air for a long moment before the last note fell like a star falling.

"Midnight," said Gideon.

The cow kneeled.

And, down in the village, just at the same moment, Dorrie's candle flickered and blew out.

# CHAPTER TEN

THE REVEREND LAPP was mightily pleased about the candle-walking. Not a flame had stayed alight in the whole procession, and he hoped that his congregation would accept this as a sign. Little Fox Jones, who was in one of his states of redemption, announced that the Reverend Lapp's eloquence had produced such a great wind that the candles were snuffed like sparks on water.

This was an attractive theory, much discussed, and most of the villagers were willing to have lost their wishes for the sake of such powerful lungs in their preacher. Dorrie, however, took no comfort and was so cast down in her spirits that Miss Emma insisted on dosing her with green–herb tonic and Miss Maidy gave her the second-best pincushion. Dorrie became ashamed and smiled, but there was a cloud over her heart.

She thought that if she could see Gideon it might ease her, but there was no excuse for calling on Mrs. Briggs, who was busy enough no doubt with all the children and the house and Gramma to care for, and Micah had not been around.

December dragged out, cold and doleful, and on its last day Dorrie got out all the makings for three Eve-cakes, one for the

Reverend Lapp, one for the Reverend Birdsong, and one for her own house. The Eve-cakes were stiff with hickory nuts and as hard as a flint-man's heart, but they carried well in the pocket and brought blessings for the New Year through some affinity with the January saints.

Miss Maidy, coming to help crack the nuts which had been laid down since squirrels' gathering time, sat herself at the kitchen table and examined the shallow bake tins, inside and out. "Dorrie," she said suddenly, "mightn't you make four without skimping?"

"With a handful more flour and nuts," Dorrie agreed. "Who would be getting it?"

"The Briggs family?" said Miss Maidy on a questing note. "It's hard for Mrs. Briggs, Mr. Briggs wandering. And Gideon's a nice lad."

Dorrie looked down at the table top, hands very busy and cheeks very pink. So, thought Miss Maidy delightedly, Emma was right.

" 'Twould be kind," said Dorrie about the cake.

"It will give you some bother, of course," said Miss Maidy cleverly. "Making the cake and then taking it to them. We could send it by the Reverend Birdsong perhaps—"

"Oh, it's no bother," said Dorrie, tongue tripping over the words. "I could take it tonight."

Miss Maidy shook her head. "There's a storm coming," she said. "Puss has been twice his size all day, and my bones do nothing but ache. Do stay young, Dorrie, it's so much more comfortable."

"Oh, dear Miss Maidy," said Dorrie, most distressed, "you shouldn't be doing the hickory nuts."

"I like it. You can take the Eve-cake tomorrow, Dorrie, and

have a visit too." She made a little innocent humming sound and put a large nut into the jaws of the old iron nut breaker. "You could go tonight, of course, if it stays clear, but I mistrust it very much and the dark comes so early."

"It might be clear," said Dorrie hopefully, feeling tomorrow very far off, whole dawn and sunset away.

"Puss thinks not," said Miss Maidy decidedly.

Puss turned out to be right, as Puss so often was. The clouds began to gather early in the afternoon, hurrying in from the west. By evensong, under a gray lit sky, the world was hissing and alive with sleet, and the wind was caging outside the village doors.

Dorrie stood at the window, looking out. It was usually her favorite time of the night, just before the curtains were pulled, when the lamp in the window and the fire on the hearth hung together in the branches of the big elm outside. But this night, just before the New Year's coming, she sighed and closed the curtains, thinking tomorrow so distant.

Miss Emma and Miss Maidy nodded their heads wisely at each other and sighed a little too, thinking what a small thing their Dorrie had been when she came to them and thinking that now she was a young woman with a heart of her own.

Miss Emma talked of her childhood, a thing she was apt to do at the year's end, and Miss Maidy fidgeted gently. After a while, Miss Emma saw the yawns struggling not to be seen and said, "There, I've talked all night and it's past bedtime," and they got up and looked at each other with sober, wide eyes and wished each other the grace of the coming year.

Dorrie smiled because she loved them very much and climbed to her room with her shadow slipping ahead of her, candlelight at its heels. When she was all ready for bed, very dignified and quite eclipsed in her nightdress and with her hair in a heavy braid down her back, she kneeled for prayers and said them very long and carefully, the year going out and so much to be remembered. But, when she finished, instead of jumping under the bright patchwork quilt as soon as her candle was blown, she went to the window and stood looking out, just as she had stood earlier in the parlor.

"Blessed be the night," said Dorrie very softly but not so soft she wouldn't be heard, "and make the day clear." She put her face to the glass and stared out but there was nothing to see. A cold shiver hurried over her, there in her bare feet with frost on the window glass, and she ran and jumped into bed and pulled her quilt up under her nose and fell asleep, all on the instant.

Outside darkness stayed, darkness and snow and ice, as if it would stay forever.

So no one in Greenwillow was prepared for the morning when it came, not in a slow snowy dawn but with the sun shouting up over the hill and catching a million mirrors of ice storm, as if the music from a harp had been frozen and splintered and flung from the west and the east and the north and the south. The great trees were sheathed in ice, and so were the tiniest meadow grasses. Branches glittered and cracked under their frozen weight, and small autumn seed-coats turned to diamond stuff.

The sky was as blue as the first dawn itself, the one that woke Adam, and there was a fresh powdering of snow that had fallen before the ice began to creep. It was next to impossible to look abroad for the dazzle, and the Reverend Birdsong stood on his doorstep and shielded his eyes and felt very near to bursting with God's wasteful glory and this new Creation.

Charity the cat came out beside him, walking very daintily in the cold, looked at the snow, sneezed in protest and withdrew to the warm hearth. Birdsong rubbed his hands together and crowed.

As he might have known it would, this brought the Reverend Lapp out on the neighbor doorstep, long-faced and disapproving, with his eyes screwed up tight against all the glitter. Ministers of the cloth, said his thin reproachful black, were not meant to crow.

"*Benedicite*," said Birdsong perversely, and then bethought him that it was wrong to annoy his fellow clergyman and said, "Good morning," instead. "What a morning for the New Year!"

"The trees will all break," said Mr. Lapp, his natural turn of mind being on the side of chaos.

"We shall have firewood," said Mr. Birdsong, being more bright than need be.

Mr. Lapp growled and stamped back into the house, where he was greeted by his mother announcing a stoppage in the chimney flue. She believed it to be caused by a storm-caught owl. Since the owl is known to be the Devil's bird, this news put heart into Mr. Lapp and gave him a feeling of wrestling with evil powers at first hand. Even the poking down of a handful of musty leaves and a dislodged chimney brick failed to discourage him from the feeling that the subject of his sermons was at large again. Quite possibly called up by Birdsong's Latin. He was even able to listen with tolerance to his mother's dissertation on what he had done to the hearthrug.

Birdsong, meanwhile, was suffering from remorse. He had truly not meant to open the New Year, a holy time, on a note of provocation, even if his neighbor had been an affront to the landscape. "Oh, dear," said Birdsong humbly and was briefly cast down, but the sight of Dorrie, stepping out into the bright world in a red cloak and with a basket on her arm, snuffed his conscience and lit his heart. He hailed her with all the enthusiasm he had been busy putting into his repentance.

Dorrie curtsied and explained her errand, and Mr. Birdsong looked pensive at the thought of food going somewhere else. "There's a cake for you, Reverend," said Dorrie, hastily, "which Miss Maidy will be bringing. And a cake for the Reverend Lapp, which Miss Emma will take to him."

"Why not the other way round?" said Mr. Birdsong inquisitively.

Dorrie understood his point. "Mrs. Lapp's always asking after the hen-cozy, and Miss Maidy gets bothered answering. Miss Emma's so much more—"

"Yes, she is. *Much* more," said Mr. Birdsong. "Well, it's a fine day for carrying Eve-cakes about."

"You'd best go inside, sir," said Dorrie anxiously. "You'll catch a death."

"God bless you," said Birdsong, sneezed tremendously and vanished in response to a cry from Mrs. Likewise, inside the house.

Dorrie shook her head and hurried off, stepping along lightly under the blue arch of sky, the sun shining through glass bushes in a glitter of broken light, and now and then the crack of a branch giving under the ice's load.

Down the road she went, and along the river which was scarcely paler than the sky, running between snowbanks and with the willows like frozen fountains. When she turned off into the meadow, there were tiny starred tracks in the snow where field mice had danced and a necklace of patterns where some wintering bird had looked for seed.

It was shorter to the Briggses' house to stay in the meadow way but Dorrie heard the frosty ring of an axe and it seemed to her, though she could not be sure, that it might be Gideon at work in the clearing. Holding the basket out stiffly in front of her with both hands, as if it must be first through the door and introduce her, she turned onto the narrow footpath. A thin spiky branch reached out and snatched at her hood, so it fell back, and a bit of hair that should have been tucked in and smooth blew against her cheek. Her cheeks were pink and her eyes were bright with her heart pounding so loud for some reason that you might think there was March thunder in the January cold, and her cloak was as scarlet as a redbird.

It wasn't any wonder that Gideon, straightening up from the tall swing of an axe stroke, felt his breath catch.

"I've brought you an Eve-cake," said Dorrie, which was foolish because the Eve-cake was for all the Briggses and not just Gideon alone.

"That's kind, Dorrie," said Gideon, suddenly minding his manners. "So early too. Would you sit on a log?"

"Of course." She looked down into the basket as if something important was going on inside it.

He brushed the snow off a downed linden tree. The bees had swarmed in its nectar-blossom only last summer and, when it went, it had splintered and toppled without warning. "You'll be warm enough?" he asked.

"Oh, yes." She put her basket down beside her and leaned forward a little, chin on fists, to watch him. After a moment he picked up the axe again, and its edge rang ice on ice. "Just the branches left to do," said Gideon, half to himself.

Dorrie nodded and looked around her. She couldn't remember ever having been in the clearing in midwinter, knowing it best in spring when she came to find flowers for Miss Maidy, violets tucked into moss by the tree roots, windflowers and bluebells, and even occasional lords-and-ladies wearing their spotted hoods. There were little saplings in the clearing, and the very big, very old trees stood about in a circle with the sky open above them. There was one empty place where a great oak had fallen, and its going had left a doorway for the sunset and a window for the gentle meadow and the hills that lay beyond.

It came to Dorrie, sitting on her log, that here would be a place to build a little house with maybe a honeysuckle vine walking across the doorway that looked at the sun. Dorrie was partial to honeysuckle vines and would plant them anywhere for the bees and the ladybugs, but the ones she brought from the woods to root by the kitchen had languished, not at home perhaps with tansy and cabbages.

She looked up quickly at Gideon and, for only a moment, she pretended that she was looking at him through her own kitchen window, waving to him just before she set the day's loaves to rise, fair and round under the white cloths.

Gideon looked back at her questioningly, and Dorrie blushed almost as bright as her cloak and gazed down at her hands.

"Are the kittens well?" said Dorrie, quickly so he couldn't look inside her thoughts.

"Turning into cats," said Gideon. "The lame one?"

"Learning nicely." She would not look at him. The little house she had dreamed kept rising around her, so near to his family and the farm and yet such a close place for two people to live together. A terrible yearning overtook her, and she pressed her hands against her heart.

Gideon drove the axe into the chopping block and left it quivering there while he bent and gathered the branches and faggoted them together.

"Is the cow well?" said Dorrie, looking at his bent head.

"She'll calve in March," Gideon said, and added, "God's mercy," having worried a good deal about it.

Dorrie said timidly, "Gideon, must you give the cow back to Mister Clegg and the calf too?"

"They're his," Gideon said shortly, then saw how troubled she looked and added, "Likely we can keep both the cow and the young one till June, when Ma's time comes. That's milk for her when she needs it." He swung his bundle of faggots to his shoulder and stood looking straight ahead for a moment. Then he said, "Mister Clegg will have full pasture by that time, and the caring will be easy enough. Perhaps, the winter after, he'll let Micah keep the cow again."

"Micah?" said Dorrie, helplessly knowing what he meant.

"Surely my call will have come by then," said Gideon.

She turned her face up to him.

"Dorrie, don't look so," he said painfully. "I've got no choice."

She pulled her cloak tighter about her. "Must you go, Gideon, when here's so much to stay for? What's out in the world that isn't in Greenwillow?" She held her hands up, cupped, as if they were holding Gideon's future. "You could build a little house, here in the clearing, near to all but maybe with someone—"

Gideon frowned, puzzled. "Who would I build a house for, Dorrie?"

"You'll—wed, likely," said Dorrie in a small voice.

Gideon shook his head. "No, Dorrie, I'll not wed. When my

call comes, I'll not do what my father did and his father before him. I'll not go to the other end of the earth with a wife waiting at home that needs me, and maybe a young thing on its way."

"A wife wouldn't mind," said Dorrie, her voice so little now that it was no more than a whisper. "She'd wait."

He stood, gazing down at her until she drew up her hood but continued to sit there unmoving, her hands in her lap and just the curve of her cheek and her round chin for him to see. For no reason, for no reason in the world, tears sprang suddenly into Gideon's eyes.

He said, "Dorrie?" and she still didn't move. Something about her made him ache inside himself, but "I'll not wed" he said again.

She stood up and, when she spoke, he thought she was angry with him because her voice was like the snow around her. He couldn't know how ashamed she was for having said so much and so forwardly. Yet it was true something inside her was angry at him, so sure he was and so possessed by his call. Could he not stop his ears against it?

"I'll be going," said Dorrie with all the dignity she had left. "You'll give the Eve-cake to your family?"

"But you'll come back with me and give it yourself?' said Gideon, distressed.

"Miss Maidy and Miss Emma will be wanting me," Dorrie said, making it plain that there were those who did and feeling her cheeks hot and tears pricking with the desire to run away and hide. What had possessed her to talk so? It was the little clearing with its shape of a house waiting, and Gideon being so near and at work.

"Please come to the house, Dorrie," Gideon said. "There's

Micah and Sheby will be wanting to show you things, and Ma, and the kittens have grown—"

"Thank you," said Dorrie very politely, "but I'll not." She put the Eve-cake into his hands and turned and walked away from him out of the clearing, feeling quite proud of herself for all of a half mile, and after that finding her pride very heavy to carry home.

Gideon watched her go, red cloak finally lost entirely among the trees, and then he shouldered his branches again and took them and the Eve-cake home. It was not until much later that he remembered the axe, left behind in the chopping block, and sent Micah to fetch it. Micah was pleased to find the clearing full of someone else's footprints and he believed it to be a wood soul, there being many about, until he realized it must have been Dorrie, bringing the cake.

He fitted his shoe into her shoemark and wished that she had come to visit the kittens and the cow, even the pig. He liked Dorrie very dearly, and it was quite a pity that she did not belong to him. But there it was, it was Sheby who belonged to him, and a great nuisance too, while Dorrie belonged to Miss Emma and Miss Maidy, as the cow belonged to Mr. Clegg. All was badly arranged.

Micah blew out his cheeks and scowled, and then he forgot the whole matter in the task of tugging the axe loose. Gideon had struck it in very deep.

# CHAPTER ELEVEN

GRAMMA BRIGGS had been biding her time, a thing she did very poorly, not having a patient soul.

She was as set as a broody hen in her determination to call on Thomas Clegg, but she knew very well that the whole family would tell her not to and, much as she enjoyed a good fight, this was one she might lose.

All she asked was for the Briggses to go and fall into the boggle's well and stay in it long enough for her to visit the old man and tell him to give Gideon the cow. She had no idea how she was going to get Christian charity into a heathen head, but that could be worked out later. What she needed now was some way to shake loose of the monstrous number of Briggses who surrounded her.

She mumbled and scowled and chewed over the problem all through January and had about decided to give it up until spring came, scattering Briggses outdoors along with the hatching tadpoles and birds fussing and house-straws. Then, on the last day of the coldest month, the Reverend Lapp arrived, coming to call with his high black hat and long face.

He said that Thomas Clegg was low, very low indeed. "It is

the Devil's victory," he said angrily. "He will not confess his sins and has set himself against the call to grace. Prayer will not prevail with him."

"Poor Mrs. Clegg," said Martha. "She's so feared he'll die without the consolations."

"He'll go straight to hell, riding on the Devil's pitchfork," said Gramma enthusiastically, and then suddenly bethought herself that this would scarcely fit her own plans. She gave her chair a jerk to get nearer to the reverend and woke the dog Rip, who was sleeping under it triumphantly after routing a clowder of cats. "Rev'rend, Thomas Clegg ain't really dying, is he?"

"There's been little change this week past," the Reverend Lapp said heavily, "and he may linger, but I fear his final days are drawing upon him."

"Dear Lord," said Gramma, reaching for her turnip to support her, "I hope it ain't so."

"Your concern does you credit," said Lapp, honestly surprised and feeling that his influence might yet provide spiritual guidance for the old lady.

"I'm real Christian," said Gramma complacently. "I was raised right. Used to go to church when I was a young un, Rev'rend, but I couldn't stand all the preachin'." She stared crossly at her turnip, which someone else had been chewing. "No offense, I hope," she added absently.

"None offered, none taken," said the Reverend Lapp, sounding a trifle vexed, and he rose. "By the way, has my colleague been here recently?"

"Your what, Reverend?" said Martha.

"Birdsong," said Lapp shortly.

"Now there's a nice fat man," Gramma observed. "I must say I like a man with meat on his bones."

The Reverend Lapp opened his mouth, closed it again and bowed himself icily out, falling over Obadiah and Jabez on the threshold. Jabez shrieked, and Gramma crooned, "Come to my buzzom, Jabby. I'll take care of ye."

Obadiah clutched excitedly at his mother. "Ma, they's a hedgehog down in the hollow, Shadrach near caught it and it bit him. Micah says he'll swell up and die from the bite. Will he, ma, will he?"

Gramma scratched her front, bothered by a crumb of ragged-cake which had missed its way. "More likely the hedge-hog'll die," she said helpfully. "Briggses is pure pizen."

"Hush up, ma." Martha crossed her arms and looked dreamy. "You know, I ain't seen a hedgehog since Amos found a little un cryin' for its mother down in the meadow. Brought it home, Amos did, and we kept it till late summer."

"Where was I?" said Jabez jealously.

"Unborned."

Jabez looked respectful. Gramma, gazing innocently at her toes, said, "Girl, whyn't you go out and see the hedgehog, they ain't so common no more. Used to be thick as bee swarms."

"Where'd they go?" said Obadiah.

"Died, and come back boggles," said Gramma with authority. "Anybody knows that."

"I thought 'twas the other way round," Martha said.

"Oh, get along with you, allus arguin'." Gramma flapped her black skirt at the three of them. "Hedgehogs don't wait, and you know you're pinin' to see the thing. Mebbe it's your little un grown big."

"Be awful old," said Martha doubtfully, but she looked excited and picked up her shawl. Jabez wiggled as if his skin didn't fit and began to gabble dramatically, waving his hands.

"Git," said Gramma, and scuttled them out, with Rip at their heels.

Once shut of relatives, she moved as fast as a hedge-sparrow, wrapping up nicely in the woolly shawl that she slept under. It was a great pity there was no time for changing into the meeting-dress, but she was not sure she could have managed it by herself anyway. Thomas Clegg would have to do without its splendor.

There was a pair of Gideon's boots in the woodbox, and she put them on, finding them large and clumpy on her feet. Her old fingers had a fearful time getting them fastened, but when the family missed her they would have nothing better to track than Gideon's boots in the snow, and this cleverness pleased her greatly.

Martha's only bonnet, tied insecurely under her chin, finished her costume nicely, and she let herself out the door, taking a quick look round to be sure no Briggses were hanging from the roof with the icicles, ready to drop down her neck. It was Gramma's experience that her kinfolk were almighty quick at comings and goings, and she just hoped the hedgehog kept them busy for a good long time.

Wrapping her shawl high around her nose and ears and pulling her heavy shirt up above snow level, she set off across the field at a sort of trot. Gideon's boots took a good deal of picking up and putting down, the snow got inside them, and the air was as cold as a frog's paws, but just the feeling she was misbehaving set her up.

The last bit of the journey was hard to manage, and Gramma snuffled a good deal inside her shawl and breathed in a lot of wool. Even so, when she got to the Clegg's door, she still had plenty of strength left for hammering on it and for shaking her skirt down around her ankles so she looked like a lady going to meeting even if it wasn't her meeting-dress.

Mrs. Clegg came just as Gramma was about to kick the door. She peered around its corner like a fieldmouse and gave a squeak when she saw who it was. "Mrs. Briggs!"

Gramma managed a sedate bow which put the whole visit on an elegant level, and then she pushed through the doorway and skimmered across the kitchen floor to the big iron stove, where she upped her skirt above Gideon's boots and felt the heat melt into her old bones.

"Surprised to see me, ain't you?" said Gramma, perceiving that the fieldmouse still huddled and sniffing with mild contempt for such a lorn creature. "I've come to call on Thomas."

Mrs. Clegg said in a thin anxious voice that her husband was not well.

"Of course he's not well," snapped Gramma. "Why'd I come to visit him on his deathbed if he was well?"

"He's real low," said Mrs. Clegg, just above a whisper. "I've sent Tattery for one of the reverends."

Gramma clucked, having no wish to share the bedside. She unwound her shawl and dropped it on the settle, rubbed her cold dry hands together and said, "Well, don't stand gawping. Take me to him."

"I don't—" said Mrs. Clegg hesitantly.

"Take myself," said Gramma and flounced past her. Mrs. Clegg burst into tears and collapsed on the settle with her face buried in her hands.

"Can't blame her," said Gramma, barging giddily into the parlor and then backing out. "Do it myself if I'd lived with Thomas Clegg all these years. Poor mealyboned thing, can't tell whether she's glad or sorry that he's a-going— Ha!" She had found the room she sought, door ajar, heavy breathing on its other side.

She went in and found herself looking straight at Thomas Clegg, propped up on his pillows, with his eyes shut. Gramma leaned on the brass footrail and stared at him for a long time, remembering a younger Thomas who had followed her through the meadow and said he would drown himself in the Meander. "Likely better if he had," said Gramma briskly aloud, but she felt sad for a moment, all the young green days and the gay girls and the begging men.

She spoke soft. She said, "Thomas, Thomas Clegg," the way she might have said it to wake up sleeping Jabez. His face twitched and his sunken mouth sucked at the air. "Thomas!" said Gramma louder, she not being one to wait.

He opened his eyes then, dry lids almost rustling and heavy with his age, and he saw her down at the bottom of the bed where his wife should have been. He said thickly, "Where's she?"

"Grieving in the kitchen," said Gramma. "I've got business to do with you, Thomas Clegg. It's about the cow."

"Eh-ah," said Thomas Clegg, letting his breath go.

"You mind me," Gramma told him severely. "I'll not be put off. The cow will do you no good where you're going, and her calf neither. Gideon's smoothed her and bedded her and given her all her needs, and she's over them staggers now and, come March, she'll bring a healthy calf."

He closed his eyes.

"Are you listening?" said Gramma.

He turned his head on the pillow, and she shrugged. One ear closed off, the other would do. "I want you to give that there cow to Gideon, Thomas Clegg. It's owing the boy, and there's two cows yet in your stable. Your wife don't need more'n the two."

He turned his head back and started sucking at the air again, for all the world, Gramma thought suddenly, like a baby that's weaning. He said something breathily, and she couldn't hear it and came around to the bedside, leaning over him. "What'd you say, Thomas Clegg? What'd you say?"

"Help me sit up," he told her, gasping like a trout out of water, his scrawny fingers clutching at the bedclothes. "Tell you—" he said.

"What you want to tell me?" said Gramma eagerly. "You want to tell me Gideon's to have the cow and the calf, too, when it comes? That's what I've come to hear."

"Tell you," said Thomas Clegg again, and she bent over him with her ear close to his thin-breathing mouth and her whole self listening. "Want to sit up, don't matter." His voice came out a little stronger, and Gramma backed off a bit. "I'll give my cow to nobody," said Thomas Clegg. "I've lived my way, and I'll die my way." He made a feeble angry move with his hands, brushing at cobwebs in a dark wood.

Gramma stared at him, dismayed. She had never imagined herself being refused, and when he closed his eyes with a terrible deep sigh and fell back against the pillows, settling into sleep or something like it, she was furious.

"Listen, Thomas Clegg," said Gramma, "you stay awake. You pay me some mind, old Thomas. I've come traipsing through snow up to my knees just to let you save your soul by giving Gideon his cow. Likely caught my death, I have. All the way back too, I've got to go, and the wind coming up and maybe a tempest. They'll find me stretched cold on the doorstep, and what'll I say to Gideon?" She gave a little angry jump. "Baby's coming in June and we're needing the cow's milk, and Gideon's going away and wants to leave a calf behind. What good's a cow where the Devil's sending you, Thomas Clegg, old man? What good's—"

He didn't answer her by so much as a flicker of the papery eyelids, his face impassive as an old owl. Gramma drew in her breath and remembered her manners. Honey, Gramma reflected suddenly, catches more flies than vinegar.

"Thomas," she said, "you mind when we was a young pair? It comes to me now that maybe I was flipperty in those times, but I was good-hearted toward you allus. You remember that, don't you, Thomas?"

Still he would make no answer, and she leaned above him, feeling a pain in her back and scolding the winter weather and the mean cold that had put it there but not losing her clutch on the problem of the cow. "Thomas," said Gramma. "Thomas?"

He was very quiet, and maybe it was his way of answering. All the old days were gone, the young ones courting in the meadow just as dead as if the meadow grass smelling of flowers had been cut down and heaped on their graves. "Past's all gone, eh, Thomas?" said Gramma and, moved by a pity for which she was not at all prepared, she reached out and touched his withered hand as it lay on the bedclothes.

She knew then why he had been so quiet. Thomas Clegg was dead.

"Thomas," said Gramma for the last time and stood there looking at him. Slipped away from her, he had, gone off by himself, and all his cows no more good to him now than the bedclothes. Gramma's face crumpled up a little, but she told herself she had seen too many dying to be sniveling over Thomas Clegg and likely it was good riddance.

She scratched her chin and looked down at all that was left of him and thought that he looked kind of comfortable.

"Go tell his wife," Gramma admonished herself, smoothed down her skirts and was about to do her duty when a stamping and a shuffling and a sound of voices outside informed her that the reverends were come. Reverend Lapp wasn't going to rejoice when he found out that Thomas Clegg had made off in the Devil's company. Nobody was going to be pleased, not Gideon, not Mr. Lapp, not the cow, not even Mr. Birdsong. Poor Mrs. Clegg, too, hoping her husband would die consoled.

It was all wrong somehow.

Gramma put her head on one side, thinking how wrong it all was and stretching her neck like some old bird.

After a moment, "What's the harm?" said Gramma, speaking to the air.

She smoothed her hair and her skirt and walked to the door in a posture of respectable holiness, a decent grief nicely mingled with a look of uplift. It was fortunate that she met the two reverends and Mrs. Clegg on the threshold, because it was a complicated expression, hard to come by and harder to keep.

Gramma singled out Mrs. Clegg for her news. "Your man's gone," said Gramma and stepped aside so they would see Thomas Clegg on his narrow bed.

Mrs. Clegg gave a cry and flung her apron up over her face. The Reverend Lapp let a long sigh slip through lips folded against despair. The Reverend Birdsong shook his head and said, "Oh, dear, dear," sadly.

Gramma put her gnarly hands together in a prayerful way and raised her eyes to the roof. "He died," said Gramma firmly and clearly, "in the peace of the Lord."

They all looked at her, Mrs. Clegg coming out from behind

her apron to do so. Gramma drew inspiration from their attention, and she nodded piously. " 'Twas like this," said Gramma.
"We was a-sitting together, and he minded the old days when
he was young. They was tears in his eyes," she added and
glanced quickly to see if this seemed too unlikely. Satisfied they
were believing her, she went on, "So we was just a-sittin' and a-
talkin' when I noticed a change comin' over him." She paused
dramatically.

"He was dying," said the Reverend Lapp, intoning like a
church bell.

If there was one thing that vexed Gramma more than
another, it was someone taking her story away from her. She
gave him a hard look. "He was a-dyin'," said Gramma grudgingly, "and he knowed it." She then took heart, seeing there
were no more interruptions. "Pray for me, he says," she
announced, coming out very powerfully with this astonishing
news.

Mrs. Clegg gave a cry of happiness.

Gramma held up her hand, always hushing people seemed
like. "I kneeled by him, and we prayed. We prayed together," said
Gramma.

"Blessed be the name of the Lord," said the Reverend Lapp.

"Amen," said the Reverend Birdsong.

It was just like being in church, without the sitting still.
Gramma felt fine. "He said to me, Thomas Clegg did," she went
on, "that he was a miserable sinner and he would go straight to
hell. Thomas Clegg, I said to him, not a sparrow falleth but the
Lord takes it into His fold. The tears stood in his eyes," said
Gramma richly.

"And then he died?" said the Reverend Lapp.

She gave him a look of real dislike, the most important part of her story still untold. "I'm coming to that, Rev'rend," she said with dignity. "We finished praying, and Thomas Clegg lifted up his eyes and he said to me that he was a-going and he knowed it but he wanted to make things right. Tell Gideon, he says, that I want to leave him the cow what he's cared for so tenderly." Gramma darted a very sharp look at Mrs. Clegg, but she was only standing there attentively, a tear running alongside her nose.

"Quite proper," said the Reverend Lapp eagerly.

"And then when he'd said that," Gramma continued with great unction, "he gave a cry. The Devil's loosin' his hold on me, he said, I see the hosts of the Lord, all gold. And then," said Gramma with sudden inspiration, "I leaned over and I said, Thomas, them that wrestled for your soul has won their battle. Meaning you, Rev'rend," she explained to Lapp.

"And then?" said the Reverend Lapp exultantly. "What did Thomas Clegg say then?"

"He said Amen," Gramma told him, "and he closed his eyes and breathed his last."

While they stood there, the Reverend Lapp seemed to grow so that the room became crowded with his bigness. He strode to Thomas Clegg's bedside and stood for a long time, looking down at the old face, before he pulled up the sheet and made the sign of the cross.

"My work has not been in vain," he gloried. "I have fought the Devil and won a victory. Let us pray together."

He kneeled, with the Reverend Birdsong beside him. At the foot of the bed, Mrs. Clegg sobbed gently, but not like she had sobbed in the kitchen, all lost and wild.

Gramma's bones were too old for bending, but it seemed disrespectful to the Lord not to thank Him for putting His words in her mouth. She went down on her creaky knees very slowly, fitted her hands together in prayer and said under her breath, for herself and the Lord alone, "Thanks be. Gideon's got the cow."

She bowed her head. Sudden sleepiness swept over her and she was going to need help getting off the floor and she missed her turnip. But, on the whole, the Lord had been very good to her today.

# CHAPTER TWELVE

MR. CLEGG was laid away the Sunday after he died, light in the coffin that Mr. Chessy had made for him. The ground lay open and cold in the church-yard, and around it the gray headstones thrust up through the melting snow, crooked and lurching and all with winter-moss fingers streaking across them.

The Reverend Lapp preached a sermon that chilled the February wind with the Devil's nearness and then warmed it with the Lord's bright victory. The church bell tolled over his head, committing the dust to the dust, but the Resurrection of the Lord beat its holy wings above the burying ground and the mourners cried "Amen" to the wonderful account of Thomas Clegg's escape from the Devil's hold.

The whole congregation was united as it had not been for years. Aggie Likewise lifted up her voice right alongside of Mrs. Lapp as if the matter of her cats' souls had become unimportant compared to the splendor of Mr. Clegg, that crochet and miser and blasphemer who had redeemed a sinful life and died peaceful in the Lord.

Mrs. Clegg, in her widow black and holding tight to the

boy Tattery's arm, paced very slow and mournful but with great dignity, and even Tattery's nose seemed less blue in this new sunshine of the Lord's approval.

Grandma Briggs was greatly missed. Her triumphant but damp journeying abroad had sat heavy on her chest, and she had been made to stay home by the fire, dosed with coltsfoot and ginger tea and wheezing with self-satisfaction. Gideon, Micah and Sheby had gone to the burying, each carrying a small sheaf of dry timothy to lay on the coffin as a mark of respect from the Briggs family and from the cow, who now slept in a shed that was hers forever.

When the heavy clods of earth rained down on Mr. Clegg, sealing him off from Greenwillow, Micah bowed his head with the rest of the congregation and shut his eyes tight. The prayer for the dead rose around him, humming quietly like bees at a honeypot, but he did not know the words and he scorned Sheby's deception of silently moving lips. After a moment, he opened his eyes a slit and darted a look around to see who had come and been missed by him.

There was Mr. Lunny, for instance, with his little dog pressed close against his leg, ears and tail standing very high and too lively a look for a burying. Micah briefly regretted not bringing Rip, but the old dog would only have taken the open grave for signs of a badger run and the excitement, though pleasant, would have been unseemly. Micah sighed and opened his eyes a bit more to look wider around him.

There was Mr. Chessy, the carpenter, large and fierce. And just behind Mr. Chessy, which was probably why Micah had missed seeing her earlier, there was Dorrie, very prim and unfamiliar in a bonnet and dark cloak. Dorrie had not come visiting to them lately, and Gideon, when asked why, had no answer.

"Blessed are the dead who die in the Lord," said the congregation, and then "Amen" and then opened its eyes. Micah closed his rapidly to show he had been praying too and just gone on a little more holy than most.

The grave now belonged to Mr. Clegg. The mourners left it slowly, moving away among the headstones and the moss, up the cobbled path and back into their own lives, all saying what a fine burying it had been and nodding in approval of the Reverend Lapp's great victory over the Devil.

Micah let loose of Gideon's hand and ran to Dorrie, with Sheby on his heels and vexed at being second. "Gramma took sick in her chest and like to die," said Micah, enlarging on the truth which was so often not as impressive as it ought to be. He then added, "Though she's better now" and also "Thanks be to God," in case the Lord might be listening. "You'll come and visit with her a bit, won't you, Dorrie? Ma said to bring you back with us."

"She did?" said Dorrie, wishing to be eased in her heart but glancing first to Gideon, who had come up and was looking very hard at the carved gray words on a headstone.

"The baby's growing very big inside Ma," said Sheby persuasively, "and the cow comes to her time next month if all goes well."

"You've not seen the cow since the Lord changed Mr. Clegg's wicked heart," said Micah.

"Hush, you mustn't ever say he was wicked." Dorrie glanced quick at Gideon again, and she so much wanted him to raise his head and look at her that she suddenly decided what had gone before made little matter. Nothing had really been said in the clearing after all, and she would be a goose of a girl to let it keep her from visiting Gramma. "Shall I come,

Gideon?" she said.

"You must please yourself," said Gideon, very carefully. But then he did look up and put Dorrie foolishly in the mind of the lame kitten, and although she had felt cold dignity coming over her, it flounced its petticoats and went its way alone. She said softly, "Oh, Gideon, I'm so glad the cow really belongs to you now."

"You'll come?" said Gideon.

"In the afternoon, early," Dorrie promised, "if Miss Maidy and Miss Emma can spare me and if Mrs. Lapp is not coming to call."

"She'll not come," said Micah serenely, crossing his fingers to ward her off.

Mrs. Lapp did not come, and Miss Emma courageously said she would have biscuits for tea instead of little cakes. She and Miss Maidy would talk about the burying and Miss Maidy was planning a square pincushion (a nearly impossible thing) and it was not only convenient for Dorrie to go but really her duty. They knew Dorrie's duty was a soft side of her and felt they were behaving very cleverly in the matter, but Dorrie would have gone even if they had told her it was a sin.

She took the long way to the farm because she felt shy, but she walked it very fast because she felt eager. February sun was melting the snow and the ground was busy storing up water for the roots. An early crow cawed from the top branch of an old oak and then flew away, hoarsely warning the still woods. Dorrie skirted the clearing where she had talked so wild and walked faster than ever, so the sun was not yet low when she reached the house.

The geese rose from the doorstep in a fury and rushed at her with their white necks stretched long and such a gabble and a hissing as brought Obadiah and Shadrach and Jabez outside with a shout. Gramma shrieked happily from the hearth that the Devil was back, and this made Dorrie laugh one of her sudden rare laughs, quick and bright like a wellspring. It reached Gideon where he was out in the shed, turning over the hay; and his heart jumped as though April had seized upon it. He put down the pitchfork and came hurrying to his own doorstep like a child that had been called.

There she was with her red cloak and her laughter, but she sobered the moment she saw him, and he remembered it was Gramma she had come to visit.

Ma called for Dorrie to come out of the cold, and Gideon, after a minute, went back to his task. Dorrie's eyes followed him, but she said nothing at all.

"Here's Dorrie, ma," said Martha, unmuffling Gramma from a blanket but leaving her feet wound in well to keep her sitting there.

" 'Bout time," said Gramma ungraciously. She gave Dorrie her turnip to hold and told her to sit down. "You'll be wanting to hear how Thomas Clegg died in the Lord," she said. "Well, it's a long story and it's getting longer. I keep recollecting bits." She sneezed dryly like a cat, and the young cats on the hearth looked at her.

Martha said, "The kettle's on, ma. Why don't you wait till Dorrie gets warmed and some tea in her?"

"Where's my ginger?" said Gramma. "Where's Micah and Sheby, girl, where's they?"

"They'll come along," said Martha. "They didn't expect Dorrie so early." She moved to the stove, walking heavy with the child in her.

"Gettin' real big, ain't she?" said Gramma approvingly. "It's kicking so early it's likely another boy. Amos near kicked me to death. I was all bruised inside like a windfall pear."

"Turned yourself inside out and had a look, I suppose," said Martha mistrustfully. "Don't go giving Dorrie silly ideas, ma. She'll be getting her own young uns one of these days." She gave Dorrie a look that put Dorrie in mind of a nesting thrush and settled the cup of tea in Gramma's restless hands.

"It'll die in the dish, it's that weak," Gramma prophesied glumly. "Dorrie, why don't you and Gideon get wed?"

Dorrie blushed and turned her head away. Pretty for a moment as an apple-blossom tree, thought Martha with an ache, and said, "You hush, ma. There's plenty young men besides our Gideon would be courting Dorrie."

"Never find a better," said Gramma. "Got his own cow, too, thanks to me being so busy. Who've you got in mind that'd be as good even?" She snorted and took her turnip away from Dorrie, feeling she would not tend it well.

Dorrie looked despairingly at Martha.

"Drink your tea, ma, and take your nap," said Martha briskly, "and when you're waked up you can tell all about Mister Clegg."

"I c'd tell it now," said Gramma, diverted.

"You go to sleep," said Martha, took the cup away, tucked her up and set the chair rocking. A cloud of muttering rose like gnats under the blanket but the tea seeped down into Gramma's old toes and the hearthfire toasted her. After a while she gave a little cluck and let her turnip roll from her fingers.

Martha leaned over heavily and picked it up to lay aside on the table. "She ain't told her story yet all day, but it'll keep. The young uns can stand hearing it again, I s'pose."

Dorrie made no answer, and Martha looked at her bent

head for a moment and then sat down by the table, resting her arms on it and cradling her cup of tea between her hands. They sat so for a long time, the room quiet with their quietness, Gramma nodding, the young cats lazy in the warmth, and outside the occasional voices of the children and, once, Gideon's voice.

Dorrie put her hands in her lap and fixed her eyes on the little cradle in the corner, an edge of the blue quilt just showing. She wanted badly to talk but the words would not say themselves, even with so many things happening like the burying, the cow and the calf, the baby to come, or even the spring that would soon now be melting the snows.

After a while, Martha put down her cup. "Dorrie."

Dorrie looked up.

"There's none I'd like better for a daughter than you," said Martha gently.

Dorrie held her hands together tight and tried to make her voice sound as if she was just saying anything. "He'll not have a wife," said Dorrie.

"He wants no girl to leave waiting when his call comes." Martha pushed the cup away from her. "Dorrie, he's not like his pa. Amos asked me to wed, he told me of the call that would come and how he'd go from me without looking over his shoulder but that, once in a while, he'd be back. I was that wild in love, he could have had me without the ring or the promise to come home, but he gave me both. It's been lonely times, but there's been the babies to carry and raise, and some day I count he'll have his fill of all the places where the wind blows, and then he'll stay."

"I'd wait," said Dorrie.

"I know, lovey. You'd make a good Briggs woman, they're

used to waiting." She nodded her head toward Gramma. "She waited, but her man he never came back. Lost somewheres, they said, with a ship that drowned. Might be true, might not, maybe he's still wandering." She sighed. "Only one that didn't wait was Amos's wife afore he had me. Poor thing, seemed like she couldn't be patient enough and slipped away and took the baby with her. Gideon remembers that, you know, Dorrie."

"Yes," said Dorrie, seeing the lonesome cradle.

"It went to his heart that she died without his pa here. Amos was struck deep too when he came back whistling and found them both in the resting ground. You know where she's laid, Dorrie?"

Dorrie shook her head.

"In the clearing. Ma and I thought she ought to lie in the churchyard, but Gideon was that crazed with grief we gave him his way. He was so little. She died in the spring, Dorrie, and we put her and her baby in among the flowers."

"In the clearing," said Dorrie. She rested her cheek on her hand and looked at Martha with gray eyes. "A place for a house."

"A place for a house," Martha agreed, understanding. "Sometimes I think Gideon will not get his call, but it's only a way of my dreaming. The call always comes."

"I wished," Dorrie said suddenly. "I wished at the candle-walking, but my candle blew out."

"The call always comes," Martha said again, then stood up quickly and shook out her skirt.

A spark spat on the hearth, and a cat jumped. Gramma woke and pounced on her blanket, blaming it for bad dreams and scrabbling at it with her hands. "I heard everything you said," said Gramma accusingly. "You was telling her my story, girl, all about the Angel of the Lord and how I said to Thomas Clegg that he must confess his sins." She got loose from the blanket and kicked it onto the floor. "I forgive you," said Gramma, "because I'm very forgivin' by nature. Come here, child, and I'll tell you how it really was. First, I'll tell you how come I didn't wear my meeting-dress."

There was a hollering outside, preceding Micah who came through the door with Sheby on his heels and a fistful of winter-black thistle in his hand. "For the pig," said Micah. "Dorrie, we were at the stile, a-waiting for you, and you never came. I found thistle for the pig, but Sheby she found nothing."

"I wasn't hunting," said Sheby with scorn.

"Have you seen the cow?" said Micah. "Gideon's at the milking." He rushed to the door and discovered Gideon just coming in, with Obadiah and Shadrach and the milk pail, sweet warm foam spilling over its shining sides. "Here's Gideon," said Micah contentedly. "Gideon, we waited for Dorrie at the stile, and here she is before us. How did you come, Dorrie?"

"By the clearing," said Dorrie, not daring to look at Gideon.

Gramma made a sound of fury and shook the arms of her rocking chair. "Talk and talk!" said Gramma peevishly and turned to Gideon with her woes. "Put me to sleep with a cup of tea, she did, and now there ain't nobody will listen to hear how I wrassled the Devil."

"And threw him onto the floor," said Micah, gleaming.

"Who's telling my story?" Gramma demanded. "Me or you?"

"You," said Micah hospitably and wrapped himself into a listening ball with his chin on his knees. Sheby slipped down beside him and sat cross-legged and serious. Obadiah and

Shadrach leaned on the table near their mother, arms wound around each other and a look of hope. After a moment, Dorrie moved over to make room on the settle and Gideon sat beside her. Both of them looked straight ahead at Gramma with great attention.

Martha said, "Where's Jabez at?"

"Worrying the pig," said Gideon, this being an accepted thing.

"Shan't miss him," said Gramma. "He hollers." She gave a bounce of anticipation, then settled herself with her hands folded over her turnip and looked perplexed. "I told you something, child, how far along had I got?"

"Just to your meeting-dress," said Dorrie, "and about why you didn't wear it."

Gramma grunted. "They was out hedgehoggin', that's why. I didn't have no time afore they all got back so I went as I was, in Gideon's boots. Doing them," said Gramma firmly, "no harm. He's wearin' 'em now."

Everybody looked respectfully at Gideon's boots. "Through the snow I went," said Gramma, "great drifts, high as the house. You remember them great drifts, Gideon?"

Gideon said yes, he did, and Dorrie gave him a soft look from under her lashes.

Gramma smacked her lips. "I come to the house, Thomas Clegg's house, and I knocked at the door."

"The Devil answered," Micah cried, having already been quiet for a dreadful span of time.

"Mrs. Clegg answered," said Gramma, paying no heed, "and she burst into tears, knowing her man was going to his grave in all his sin and shame. Poor soul. Amen." She took a chaw of turnip and gazed piously at the roof. "So I went and found

Thomas Clegg, a-lying in his bed, and I sat down aside him and I said, 'Thomas Clegg, you're about to die and you ain't fit to die and—' "

The door swung open, and Jabez burst through, shrieking.

"Here's trouble," said Micah.

"Lovey," said Martha, "what you been doing?"

Jabez flung himself on her and sobbed out that he had fallen into the swill pail. "Pig kicked me," he wailed.

Gramma said, with feeling, "Wish it had et you, Jabez Briggs, come a-hollering in the middle of my story."

"Take off them clothes, Jabez," said Martha resignedly, "and I'll wrap you into a blanket. Gideon, give the fire a poke. Sheby love, find a blanket, do."

"Pig'll starve to death 'thout its swill," said Sheby, moving slowly.

"Oh, oh, oh," said Gramma, stamping both feet on the floor. "Ain't nobody cares how Thomas Clegg died! He was my oldest friend on earth, he was, and there ain't none of you cares. Left Gideon the cow, he did, a finer man never lived—Gideon, dog's a-scratchin' at the door."

Gideon got up and let Rip in, and the old dog tramped to the hearthfire and laid himself down, nose on paws, cats giving grudging room. Jabez stopped howling and Sheby found the blanket but the room, stirred up, did not settle.

Gramma drew in a tremendous deep breath like the wind on a storm-lull. She sat up very straight and looked at the wall and said in her loudest voice, and very fast, "And he said he was a miserable sinner and he repented of his sins, and then he looked outa the window and saw the hosts of the Lord a-comin', all gold, and Pray, he said, and I prayed, and then he gived me the cow for Gideon and said Amen and died." She then nodded her head fiercely, said, "There, that's how it was," and burst into tears. "No one wants to hear me out," said Gramma. "Ain't no one loves a poor old body like me."

All the Briggses turned to her, anguished, but it was Dorrie who flew from the settle and kneeled down by the rocking chair and put her arms around the small quivering old thing. "I love you," said Dorrie. "Dear Gramma."

Gramma gave a sniff and looked at her with pleased mistiness. "B'lieve you do," said Gramma.

"*I* love you," said Micah, leaning over the back of the chair and twining around her neck. "We do too," said Shadrach and Obadiah sentimentally, quite caught up in the occasion. "You c'n have all my milkweed pods," Sheby offered, "poor Gramma." "Sure, ma, we all love you," said Martha patiently and dropped Jabez down onto the bed, so rolled in his blanket that he was speechless.

Gramma made a noise like a cricket in the sun and eyed them all complacently. "C'd tell the story all over again, I guess I could. Went over some of the best bits kind of fast."

"It's supper time," said Martha, very firmly.

Dorrie jumped to her feet, looked down at Gramma who was getting stormy again and said, "Miss Emma and Miss Maidy will be watching for me. Next time I come I'll bring you a plumcake."

Gramma made a greedy sound of pleasure. Gideon said, "I'll walk you home, Dorrie, it's dark."

Micah said instantly, "May I come with you, Gideon, may I? I'll walk softer than the stars in the sky. I'll walk like a fox with its paws."

Gideon hesitated.

" 'F you don't wed that girl, Gideon Briggs," said Gramma

severely, "you're no grandson of mine. In my day, a man saw a girl who spoke so soft and made plumcake, he didn't stand about a-talkin' to his toes—"

"Ma," said Martha warningly.

Dorrie and Gideon both looked very hard at the floor. After a moment Dorrie said, "If Micah comes, you'll have someone to walk back with you, Gideon."

Gideon, speaking carefully to the cats, said that would be true. They both looked at Micah almost pleadingly, and Micah leaped like a shooting star.

When the door closed after them, Martha turned to Gramma with her hands on her hips. "What'd you want to make them so uneasy for," she said reproachfully. "Honest, ma, there's times I think you've got a tongue for every tooth you've lost."

"Allus hushing me," said Gramma loftily, and held out her arms. "Give me Jabez, girl, give me the littlest one what ain't allus hushin' his old gramma. Give me Jabez, and I'll tell him all about how the Angel of the Lord come down on a gold cloud to save Thomas Clegg's soul." She looked around, proud of this new vision, but she had lost most of her audience. "Heh," she said. "Come on, Jabez love, come hear a story."

Jabez rolled down off the bed and floundered toward her, struggling inside his blanket. "I'll tell you one, Gramma," he said breathlessly. "I'll tell you how that there pig kicked me into the swill bucket. I still smell. Smell me, Gramma." He pushed himself at her proudly.

Martha took down the boiling pot. "Likely I should've kept Micah home," she said slowly.

Sheby said, "Ma. Is Dorrie and Gideon going to wed?"

"Hush, lovey."

"There," said Gramma triumphantly. "Somebody's hushed besides me!"

# CHAPTER THIRTEEN

O N THE first night of March, a comet split the sky. Gideon, coming out of the cowshed, stared in awe at the long fierce tail of light struck across the clouds, dark with great winds and the snow blowing wild. Micah, peering from behind him, breathed "Sweet gracious!" and blew on his cold fingers.

"Likely a sign," said Micah delightedly. "We shall be having a little bull-cow." He shook his head. "Takes her very long, Gideon."

Gideon nodded. This was the second sunrise that he and Micah had stood watch over since he had gone to milk and found the cow moving her head restlessly from side to side, her bag swollen and feverish and heavy with the birth-milk. "Waiting's all we can do," he said. "I'll watch. You sleep in the hay for a bit, Micah."

"It's not needed," said Micah politely, and added, "Wind's very high."

"It will blow out," Gideon told him. "The comet falling will break the weather." He put his hand on his brother's shoulder and turned him back into the shed, away from the bitter wind and the thinning snow and into the golden circle of light snug about the lantern.

The cow was standing with her legs spread stiff and her head down, and she turned toward them without seeing or hearing. Micah's voice dropped to a whisper. "Cow's very quiet," he said.

"Yes." Gideon glanced down at his hands and hoped they would be wise when they were needed. She was such a patient cow. He leaned against the shed wall and watched the hay dust settle in the lantern light as Micah made himself a nest.

"Gideon?"

"Yes."

"When she kneeled on the Lord's night," said Micah, "would she have been praying for Jesus to get born?"

"I don't know, Micah."

"Dorrie would know," said Micah. "I must ask her. If our cow prayed for Jesus, I think Jesus ought to pray for our cow. Are you and Dorrie going to wed, Gideon? Ma said I wasn't to ask you, but who else knows?"

"You know I'll never wed, Micah."

"I'd take care of her," said Micah hopefully, "along with the cow and the calf and the pig. Sheby minds the geese."

There being no answer from Gideon, Micah sighed and curled himself more tightly into the straw. Gideon dropped beside him and sat silent, his arms wound about his knees. The lantern flame paled as light began to creep, thin and gray, around the cowshed. The wind was dying against the dawn, and there was near-quiet outside the door. After a moment, Micah slept lightly, his breath just stirring the straw.

Gideon looked down at him, so small and so anxious to take care of everybody. It was less to look after, not more, that

Micah ought to have when the call came, but a little calf would help not hinder him. A heifer would be best, thought Gideon. It could be bred to the traveling-bull in September a year away, and Micah would be on the way to a herd. Obadiah and Shadrach were growing up, Sheby more helpful to her mother. The passing years might see the little farm getting quite proud—

Gideon felt such a sudden longing go through him that he bowed his head on his knees. There would be so much happening, and he not here to see it. The seasons turning without him: autumns all coppery, winters deep and still with the snow hush, the catkin look of spring, warm summer nights and the fields lit with flowers. The children growing tall, Micah a young man, and Dorrie in her scarlet cloak likely finding someone in the village to wed. Ma alone with two men wandering, Gramma wrapping herself up in a cobweb of oldness, Sheby turned wild, turned tame?

If the call would wait! Gideon thought despairingly, knowing it would not.

Micah's hand on his knee splintered his thoughts like a stone thrown into an ice pond.

"Gideon! Look!"

Gideon raised his head and got up quickly, going to the cow. "So," he said, "so, so," and rubbed her head between the nubbed horns, feeling a tremble run all through her.

"Something's to happen," said Micah, and then scarcely had time to scramble to his feet and stand amazed.

Forefeet and nose came the little calf, struggling free from its ten-month home. The cow lowed dreadfully, and Micah shivered with a cold wind that blew like a ghost. Then suddenly, wet and asprawl, the shaky thing was out, and the cow's sides heaved in a great peace.

Gideon's hands, quick and tender, wiped the new soft nose and cut the cord between birth and life. "It's a heifer, Micah," he said and touched the cow's bag with cautious fingers. She looked at him mildly and nosed her baby, gave it a wide lick of her great tongue.

"It's wet already," said Micah, protesting.

"She's drying it. Open the door, Micah, and let in the morning."

Micah pushed it ajar and tasted the day, and a young cat edged through and sat down on the shed floor to wash its face, soft paw embracing gray ears, placid gaze fixed on the cow and calf.

"Ma must've let the cats out," said Gideon. "They were by the fire."

"I'm hungry," said Micah.

"We'll wait a bit for the new one first," Gideon said. "This will be the first meal it's ever had."

"So 'tis," said Micah, impressed, and folded his hands across his own stomach which would have to learn patience.

The calf was trying its legs already and finding them uncertain, spindly young willow sticks, not easy in a tipping world. It tottered at every swish of its mother's tongue, then insisted on four feet again until finally it was near steady.

Micah admired it loudly and said, "Now it will be drinking,"

"Wait a while," said Gideon. The hay was turning from amber to pale morning silver, and he blew out the lantern not needed now. The cat tucked its head and tidied its bib. The pig thumped in the lean-to. Time was impossibly slow.

"Soon now," said Gideon, after an endless whip. The cow

stopped its task, lifted her head satisfied, then nudged her baby, soft-nosed. The calf found the milk it had been seeking and strained at the heavy bag, sucking greedily, head outthrust and legs quivering.

"Eating time," said Micah like a mourning dove.

It took as long to get fed as to get dried, but at last the little calf sucked less greedily, lost the yielding teat, found it again with less interest. After a moment, it let go entirely and stood uncertain. "It's filled," said Micah gratefully.

"Likely it'll sleep now," Gideon said, and they watched, along with the cat, as the small, comforted, new thing curled into the soft hay and poked its nose into its flank.

"First sleep too," said Micah, collecting first occasions. He embraced the cow admiringly, and she endured him with patience. "Nobody knows except us," he said, gazing possessively around the shed. "It's true nobody knows, Sheby least of all. Poor Sheby," he said insincerely. "Gideon, can I do the telling?"

Gideon nodded and picked up the dark lantern.

"All the telling?" said Micah, still able to dance with impatience though fainting with hunger. "May I go to the village and tell whoever I meet? It's very interested, the village is. May I tell Dorrie?"

Gideon hesitated, having thought to tell Dorrie himself. "She could come and see it perhaps," he said slowly and was surprised to find how his heart ran ahead of him to her coming.

"Likely she's baking," said Micah, moving to the door.

"You're not to ask for a cake," said Gideon.

Micah turned his head to stare his astonishment at the thought. "Gideon, I never ask for such things. Not even Sheby asks for such things. Jabez does because he has no manners, but not any of the other of us. I only speak well of her little cakes, Gideon, it would not be hospitable to speak unkindly of them. Dorrie would feel so sad."

"Micah—"

"All's well then," said Micah and leaped away from his brother with the suddenness of a tree peeper, running toward the house. "Ma—Sheby—Gramma—" He speeded, shouting, spending his precious news like grain on the ground. "Cow's had her birthing. Calf's come."

It turned out, in the pearl-colored, blizzard-swept morning, that only Martha was up and moving about.

It took Micah no time at all to raise confusion—Jabez yammering, Gramma all mixed up about who had been born, Sheby furious not to have been wakened, Obadiah falling off the bed in his hurry, and Shadrach refusing to rouse at all, burrowing deep, ready to stir for nothing less than spring. Obadiah finally made the news clear to him, and, wrapped in whatever came to hand, they all trooped out into snow and ice to see the gift the cow had made for them.

"All was mine to tell," said Micah, gazing after them. Dreamily, he found a pot of honey which he himself had helped to gather and, clutching it, fell instantly asleep with his head on the table.

Gideon looked across at Martha, who smiled and said, "I'm glad the calf came well."

"Micah was quiet and good, and I'd little to do."

Gramma, understood to be asleep, spoke from her bed. "It'll be like that when your ma's time comes. No more trouble'n a flea sliding down a bedpost, that's what I said when Jabez was born and the pair. Sheby come harder, her bein' a girl. Terrible tiresome, girls is. Where's my porridge?"

Martha turned from the stove. "You want honey on it, ma? Looks like Micah figures this is a birth day."

"Honey on my porridge and in my tea," said Gramma, sucking her gums in anticipation. "Wake him up afore he pours the whole jar on top of his head."

"Porridge is hot, Micah," Martha said. "Gideon, go shout the others." She lifted a cat out of the way with her foot. "Micah, wake up, child."

Micah woke and fell on the steaming bowl and was half-way into a second helping before his kinfolk returned. He eyed them benevolently and began to describe at once, in a porridgey voice, the calf's arrival. "Come like a pit out of a plum," he said, and added casually, "They was a comet last night too, Sheby."

Sheby put down her spoon and looked at him. "You might have called me, Micah. You might."

"Not fittin'," said Micah. " 'Twas man's work."

Sheby stared at him for a long moment, then made a sound like a whippoorwill and put her head down on the table. The first sob arrested even the attention of the cats and they turned their heads, mewing questions. Obadiah, Shadrach and Jabez fixed round eyes on Micah, who cried "Sheby" in a passion of remorse and flew round the table to her side.

She hit him with her fists and howled.

"Scratch his eyes out," said Gramma helpfully.

"There," said Micah, backing off and offering consolation from a distance. "Listen, Sheby, listen to what I've to tell you." He coaxed, pussy-voiced. "We're to go to the village, Sheby, you and myself, and tell all the news. The calf was birthed and how the cow feels sad—Sheby?"

She snuffled and rubbed her nose in the crook of her arm. Micah patted her, cautiously. "Two of us is better than one to tell the news," he said, a little sadly.

Martha said, "You'll go to Mrs. Clegg first of all, Micah, before anyone. She's near kin to that calf."

"Tattery too," said Micah. "And we'll knock on the stable door and tell the cows that our cow lived with once. Might be hurt did they not know. Sheby, are you eating forever?"

She was not. She was first out the door and halfway to the meadow before he caught her up. When they came to the stile, they climbed it hand in hand, forgiving each other silently.

## CHAPTER FOURTEEN

M RS. CLEGG was still abed but the boy Tattery was rustling about inside the corncrib like a dry wind, and Micah pushed his nose and his tidings through the slatted side. "I'll come out," said Tattery and appeared with a great ear of corn in his hands, kernels like sunshine.

Sheby eyed it avidly and thought of the pig.

Tattery said, "Was there trouble bringing the calf?"

"None," Micah said promptly. "The comet was no faster. You saw the comet?"

"Sky's full of such things," Tattery said, causing Sheby much comfort. "Cow slipped her first calf, you know, Micah. Mister Clegg looked for trouble for her, which was why she was loaned."

"She's ours now," Micah said contentedly. "Tattery, will you give the news to Mrs. Clegg and to the cows? We've the village to tell."

Tattery nodded responsibly. "Don't stand about," Micah said severely to Sheby and snatched her hand. She looked back longingly over her shoulder at the ear of corn, but it went away with Tattery and no doubt the hens would be having a fine pecking out of what should have been the pig's dinner.

"Down to the river," Micah sang out, "along the river, up the street and so to Dorrie," and ran down the hill with Sheby flying after.

The Meander was in early flood after the night's wild news, and the swamp that kept it tame must have risen high about the roots of catbrier and alder and the young springing willows. The river came tumbling into the village with sticks and sprigs tossing about on it, bits of wintry sod and shreds of bark and seed wings. Ice had splintered along the banks in the thawing, and the river whirled it away, crack and spin, with the water licking cold against cold.

Sheby and Micah strayed along its margin, tranced, until just above the church they came suddenly on Little Fox Jones, tucked into the bank by a shallows, water up over his bootlaces.

"You're early about," said Micah.

"Mister Lunny's very slow about opening up his door this morning," said Little Fox Jones. "I've been waiting from before dawn, and thirst is a fearsome thing."

"Our cow birthed," Sheby said.

"There's those that like milk," Little Fox Jones admitted.

"It had a calf," said Sheby determinedly.

"Likely you thought it'd have a kitten," said Little Fox Jones and guffawed. Then he saw the blue storm rising in Sheby's eyes and repented hastily. "There, don't be vexed with an old fool, child. I'm glad you've a calf come at last. Heifer or bull?"

"Heifer," said Micah.

"Mind her close on Midsummer Eve," Little Fox Jones warned. "Stake her in mid-pasture and keep the woods away. Woods creep close, you know that, on Midsummer Eve, and there's things that want young heifers."

"We'll watch," Micah promised and, in polite exchange for this bit of learning, he inquired after the Devil.

"Visits me nightly," said Little Fox Jones, "and so does the Reverend Lapp. They don't give me no peace." He pulled his toes out of the river and eyed them closely. "River's in my boots," he remarked and returned to the Devil. "Seems like the Reverend takes more interest in the Evil One than I do, but it's only natural. The good man did well with Mister Clegg's soul."

"He died very holy," said Micah.

"God rest him," said Little Fox Jones. "I'll come along to the village with you, I think. Mister Lunny may need help with his doors." He got to his feet, and the Meander squelched in his shoes as he walked, all bits and pieces, as if he was made of twigs.

Mr. Lunny was greatly pleased over news of the calf. They left Little Fox Jones in his care, snugged down by the fire with a hopeful thirsty look, and went on to find Dorrie. She should have been told first perhaps, but it had not worked out that way.

Dorrie was in the kitchen, down on her knees, dusting the wood in the woodbox. The oven was as cold as the grave, there was no good smell of sugar and pastry, only soap, and Puss was up on top of the dresser making the blue-and-white china very anxious. The lame cat-kitten was playing languidly with the strings of Dorrie's apron.

"Dorrie," said Micah, gravely upset, "what's amiss?"

Dorrie sat back on her heels and gave them a wide vague look. Then she said "Oh" and got to her feet and, pushing a lock of hair off her forehead, said "Oh, dear" in a woeful way.

"What *is* it?" said Micah.

She smiled at him, and the kitchen turned more cheerful.

"Nothing so awful, Micah. It's a holy day and I'd planned a baking. I planned the little tea cakes Miss Emma's so fond on, but before I could even get the flour out Mrs. Lapp came poking. She said she smelled ginger cake over the hedge yesterday morning."

"Had she?" said Micah, his mouth watering.

"Ginger cake's not against Lent," Dorrie said stubbornly.

"Oh, Lent," said Micah and Sheby together, suddenly understanding and remembering that the Lord had left a great many instructions about food. "He couldn't have meant ginger cakes," said Micah, having much respect for the Lord.

"Mrs. Lapp says He did," said Dorrie, "and I'm scared of the Reverend too. He's grown so large since he won over the Devil, and Mister Clegg—Oh, Micah, Sheby! The cow!"

"That's why we've come to tell you," said Micah, recollecting. "The calf was birthed last night, about comet time. Not a bull-cow, Dorrie, but then they're most troublesome."

"I've heard that," said Dorrie. She turned and reached to take a great white crock off the shelf, and Puss sprang from the dresser top into the hole left empty. Dorrie lifted the cover and a warm spicy smell rushed out like Christmas hung on a bough of March. "I saved four gingercakes," said Dorrie, speaking very soft since there was no telling who might be counting ginger cakes over her shoulder on a holy-day. "You may have them to eat on your way home, once you're well past the church."

"It's not Lent with us," said Micah, biting off a corner to make sure it was real. "We had honey with the porridge."

"It's fine about the calf," Dorrie said.

"Gideon says you're to visit her. Could you come back with us, Dorrie? You've no baking you may do, and I think the house must be well in order or you'd not be dusting the firewood."

"It's all shined from the chimney down," Dorrie admitted. "I could think of nothing else to do but the woodbox."

"Come back with us," said Sheby, absently biting into her second ginger cake. "Do, Dorrie."

Dorrie said doubtfully, "Miss Maidy and Miss Emma went to the praying at the church—"

"We'll wait," said Micah, and added suddenly, "All the ginger cakes are gone. How too bad."

"It's no matter," said Dorrie. "I near told Mrs. Lapp there were none, and now it's true."

Sheby, her nose to the window, cried "They're coming," and flew outside, Micah flying behind her. Miss Maidy and Miss Emma, pacing up the road with holy-day properness and in the company of the Reverend Birdsong, found the two of them hanging like oriole nests from the garden gate.

"Miss Maidy, Miss Emma," said Micah and bowed to them over the pickets which stuck into him. He got down hastily and came round, still talking. "Our calf was birthed last night at comet time, and Gideon's very anxious for Dorrie to see the young thing. May she come with us? Good morning, Reverend."

"Good morning," said Mr. Birdsong.

Dorrie, coming up, curtsied to all. "I'll not go if it hinders you," she said anxiously.

"Nonsense, child," said Miss Emma. "You had already cleaned the whole house by sun-up."

"I've cleaned it again since," Dorrie said and explained to the reverend. "It being a holy-day, and no baking."

Mr. Birdsong peered at Micah's front. "I see you've been wrestling with temptation, Micah. Some of it came off on you."

"Ginger cake," said Micah promptly. "At our house it's not Lent. We had honey with the porridge."

Miss Emma clucked mildly. "Run along then, Dorrie," she said, and watched them go, with Micah and Sheby tugging Dorrie to run and she holding back, it being almost the same as a Sabbath. "Dear, dear, I'm glad the calf has come safely. Dorrie's been anxious."

"She frets because of Gideon," said Miss Maidy, and promptly turned pink.

Mr. Birdsong looked inside his hat, and there was a moment's silence while Miss Maidy gasped and recovered. Then he nodded his head and said, "It's hard on the child."

"We haven't liked to ask," said Miss Emma. "If Gideon had spoken, I'm sure Dorrie would tell us."

Birdsong eyed them both. "You'd miss her greatly if she wed."

"We could manage," said Miss Emma. "I have often assisted in polishing the silver, and Maidy makes excellent tea."

"Thank you, Sister." Miss Maidy smiled down modestly at the small toes of her church boots. "Dorrie should have her own home, of course, Reverend. We'd be only too happy for her."

Birdsong bowed. He would have liked to have given them some small gift—a meadow full of wild flowers, perhaps, or all the stars in the sky—but he was obliged to content himself with a bow. "Did you know that Gideon has said he'll never wed?"

"Oh dear," said Miss Maidy, "it's his father, I suppose. Being a wanderer. Dear, dear, how very like a man. Begging your pardon, Reverend."

Birdsong murmured his forgiveness.

Miss Emma said, "Poor little Dorrie," and a shadow fell upon them with the Reverend Lapp behind it, looking very tall and full of Lenten holiness.

Miss Maidy fluttered her hands about as if they were passing teacups in the air, and said that she had enjoyed the sermons.

"You cannot possibly have enjoyed *both* sermons," said Mr. Lapp discouragingly. He then added that sermons were not meant to be enjoyed.

"We have been rejoicing over the arrival of the Briggses' calf," said Mr. Birdsong pacifically. "It came with the comet."

"In Lent?" Mr. Lapp exclaimed.

"We were rejoicing over it," said Mr. Birdsong, a trifle testily, "not planning to eat it. Gideon was worried about the cow, and I for one am happy all went so well."

Mr. Lapp pointed his nose at heaven and put the tips of his fingers together, making of himself a pulpit. "It would be seemly in Gideon Briggs," he said austerely, "to worry more about the Devil's mastery of him and less about his cow."

"*Absit invidia*," said Birdsong with spirit, breaking his Lenten vow about vexing his colleague.

Mr. Lapp drew himself up so high that he nearly came through the top of his hat. "In matters of the Devil," he said coldly, "I think I may claim to have some experience. Good day." He bowed to Miss Maidy and Miss Emma, jerked his chin at Birdsong and walked off.

Mr. Birdsong sighed, contrition arriving too late as usual. "What am I thinking of?" he said soberly. "First, jam for my morning meal. And now this wilful use of Latin. Dear, dear."

Miss Emma looked at him sharply. "Reverend Birdsong, do you mean to tell me that you had jam this morning? In Lent?"

"I must go," said Mr. Birdsong hastily, searching about for his hat to raise and finding it on his head. "I have many duties, many duties indeed." He gave them a smile of special sweetness and hurried away.

"Really," said Miss Emma, gazing after him. "I do think if the Reverend could have jam for breakfast, there would be no harm, Maidy, no real harm—"

"One must keep up one's strength," said Miss Maidy loyally and led the way into the house, not knowing that the crock was empty and the ginger cakes were already gone.

# CHAPTER FIFTEEN

THE WEST wind brought April promise, and leaf buds opened as soft as flowers along the winter-bare branches of oak and birch and aspen. The chatter of nesting began in eaves and boughs, and the blackthorn bloomed early, snowing its petals onto the dark ground.

Golden tassels dangled from the swamp branches, and the Meander retreated into its banks. The willows hung green mist over the narrow water, and lambs came about as naturally as primroses in the short greening grass.

The little calf grew and learned to chew its cud, and Dorrie came to visit it often, other things drawing her in the same direction—the daisies in Gideon's meadow, for instance, or the bluebells lying so thick in the clearing that the sky might have fallen. Gideon found her there sometimes, sitting on the downed linden tree with her chin in her hands, not wearing her scarlet cloak any longer with spring come into the woods but in gray-blue linsey like a pussywillow.

One day she had brought him a citron bun as she had promised herself to do, and he ate it gravely down to the last crumb, thanking her so carefully that she cried out against his gratitude. "Oh, Gideon, it was such a small thing!"

"But you made it for me and you carried it," he said, and then he could see he was being foolish because a citron bun could scarcely have weighed her down. "Well, it was kind," he said.

"It was not meant for kindness," said Dorrie. "It was meant to please you."

"It did please me," he said soberly, and they sat in silence for a very long time, neither of them speaking until Dorrie remembered that she had come for a handful of flowers for Miss Maidy. He picked the ones she asked him to, kneeling to find the violets' long stem, and, having him a little way off from her, she found her tongue.

"Where will you go, Gideon?" she said.

He knew, without asking, what she meant, and he came back to her and put the flowers into her hands before he answered. "I'll follow the Meander like Pa did," he said finally.

"Where will it take you?" Dorrie asked, trying to imagine a Meander that was not Greenwillow's.

"To another river."

"A great one?"

He nodded. "Too great to cross."

"How do you know, Gideon?"

"Pa told me. Rivers lead into rivers, he said, and each one greater than the one before, until the last one opens, into a world of water. There's ships," he said.

"Where will they take you?" said Dorrie, doing her best to journey with him in her mind, thinking that a ship that took a man would bring him back some day, however far.

"There's no knowing," said Gideon.

Dorrie looked down at the flowers on her lap, thinking she

ought to be taking them back to Miss Maidy now before their dark leaves wilted, and then she looked up at Gideon, standing above her.

"Do you want more flowers, Dorrie?"

"Yes," she said to drive him away. She was remembering how forward she had been that other time in the clearing, just when the year was new and there was snow on the ground, and how ashamed that she had spoken out and let him glimpse what was in her heart, if only for a moment. But that was in January and this was April, and she was older and wiser by months, old enough to know it was no use to deny Gideon's call or try to wish it into silence. It would come, even if the Meander ran backward and the bell in the church steeple tolled without any hand to touch the bell rope.

"Gideon," said Dorrie, "I understand how it is that you have to go."

He had been kneeling to single out the widest violet-faces, but he turned and stood up. "It's not my wish, Dorrie! Do you think I'd not stay forever if only I could?"

"I know." She looked down at the roots of the tree he was standing by, moss so thick about them that the twists and gnarls were all cups of green velvet. "Gideon, at the candle-walking on Christmas Eve I used my wish against your call, though I've never told you." She raised her eyes. "The candle blew out."

"You never should have wasted your wish, Dorrie. You should have asked something for yourself."

"I *was* asking for myself, Gideon," said Dorrie.

All the violets he had picked spilled through his fingers, and their bits of sky and their heart-leaves fell and lay at Dorrie's feet. He looked at her with the west wind lifting her unbound hair from her shoulders and April all around her and the earth jubilating, everything new and winter past and no more than a step between where she sat and he stood.

He took the step and lifted her up to him with his hands at her waist that was as narrow as a birch tree and, without even thinking what he was about, he kissed her mouth. It was like tasting wild strawberries in June warm from the sun, or like lying under an apple-blossom tree and looking up through it to the summer-blue sky with the brown bees humming.

Gideon lifted his head and said, "Dorrie," and the sound of her name gladdened him so that he kissed her again.

When he finally let her go, she slipped down onto the log as if the earth was no kind of support at all, the joy in her heart being almost too great to be borne. A woodthrush overhead sang its flute song all the way through, though nobody listened, and then it flew away. The woods stood about, waiting, and the violets faded their blue on the ground. After a moment, Gideon dropped down at Dorrie's side and took her hand in his and she laid her head against his shoulder.

Now the bird had gone, and the violets, and the light was going out of the sky. There was the cow to milk and supper to lay ready and a curl of chimney smoke waiting for each of them, and still they sat until at last Dorrie said wonderingly, "All's so quiet, Gideon."

"It's always quiet here," said Gideon and lifted her hand to his cheek. "There's those that are sleeping."

She had forgotten about the burying place, but the thought of it was reassuring somehow as if Gideon's mother would be glad to see them there. The burying place would be company for her when Gideon was gone on his wandering, and she would plant a honeysuckle and primroses perhaps with their pale yellow flowers that folded at night over tiny rose-pink moths coming for nectar.

"Oh, Gideon, could we have our house here?" said Dorrie.

He looked at her unbelievingly, and she was instantly ashamed of her selfishness, asking him to build a house with spring coming on so fast, earth to be turned and seeds to be sowed and too much work to do already. "Only a hearthstone and a roof, Gideon," she said with her head bent. "Nothing grand like your house."

He saw then the wicked thing that he had let happen because of April softness and Dorrie's blowing hair and warm mouth. He dropped her hands and got up and moved away from her. "Oh, Dorrie," he said, "what have I done?"

"Gideon," said Dorrie, terrified, "don't you love me?"

"I love you," said Gideon.

She could feel her heart sigh its gratitude, and the fear left her. She smiled and went to him and took his hands. "Then all's well, Gideon, and we'll wed."

"Dorrie, no!"

"Yes, Gideon," she said peacefully. "You think it's wrong to be leaving me when your call comes, but it's not true. There will be times when you'll come back like your pa does, and then I'll be waiting for you. I'll not mind waiting all my life."

"Dorrie, listen," he said. She put her head down stubbornly, refusing to hear, until he said, "Listen, love," and then she looked up and listened. "I'll tell you what I've told no one," said Gideon. "This claim that's laid on me—"

"It's a call, Gideon, it's only a call."

"Claim or call," said Gideon, "it's done its last work." He took her by the shoulders and put her away from him, and he said, "I'll not wed, Dorrie, and then there'll be no more wanderers. The first son that comes to the first son is the wandering one, but I'll have no sons and the call will die with me. Do you understand now?"

There was a long long silence, so deep about them the green things could almost be heard to grow. Then, "I understand," said Dorrie slowly, and she did, it was true. She had come like a young foolish child to the clearing and she would go away now very grown, knowing she was loved. Between now and forever, there were many miracles that might happen, and a waiting woman could pray for them. Perhaps the Angel of the Lord would come down, like he had come to Mr. Clegg, and he would hold out his hand and his words would be, "Gideon, stay"—

"Don't be wishing, Dorrie," said Gideon, out of hard knowledge. "There's nothing can change it." And then he said very tenderly, "My little love," and there was such a burst of singing that the thrush might have come back to the bough.

But it was only Dorrie's unreasonable and hoping heart.

# CHAPTER SIXTEEN

MICAH LED the cow out to the meadow with a wreath of white-edged ditch parsley around her neck, and the May-foolish calf teetering and plunging behind. Back of the calf came the pig, complaining mightily, and back of the pig came Jabez.

Gideon was just setting the last blows to a tethering stake, where the grass was brightest, and the cow took kindly to this wide circle for wandering with the young thing to mind.

"The pig's to go where the woods fall off and the rooting's handy," Gideon said to Jabez, the very youngest Briggs having somehow arrived at a firm place in the pig's unlikely affections. Jabez nodded and spoke to the pig in a pleasant language, and the obstinate animal followed him obediently to a scratched bare place under late-leafing trees, where a shuffling snout could find much to do and Jabez could sit on a log and poke the dirt with a pointed stick.

"Ladies' Meeting today," said Micah, sitting down in the meadow to hunt for clover which would scarcely come till June.

Gideon nodded, and the cow bent her head and tried to eat

part of her wreath.

"Obadiah and Shadrach went last time," said Micah. " 'Twas at Mrs. Likewise's, and they got two sweetballs each. Here's a May-bug, Gideon." He put the bug back on its blade of grass, and it continued its placid journey up the green road. "Gideon, Sheby went the time before that to the Ladies' Meeting. It should be me to go this time. It's at Dorrie's house."

"Miss Emma's house, and Miss Maidy's."

"Dorrie cares for it. Shouldn't she have a house of her own, Gideon, like me?" He went on without an answer. "Mrs. Lapp and Mrs. Likewise, they're making a cloth for the altar, all covered with pansies, the two of them. I should be there, Gideon, because there's so much to be done, running to the church to see if the altar's a new size or should the pansies all be purple? Mrs. Likewise works at one end and Mrs. Lapp works at the other, and they talk to each other all the time. They used not to talk, you know, Gideon."

Gideon said he had heard that and asked the cow to move over.

"It was Mister Clegg's dying so holy that brought them to speak together. Mrs. Likewise said it was a great credit to the church, the Reverend triumphing over the Devil. She says he's wrong about cats, but she forgives him because the Lord will likely open his eyes some day. Do you think cats go to heaven, Gideon, May-bugs too?"

Gideon looked at him helplessly.

"The pig's not likely," Micah decided. "But Dorrie's lame kitten would be going, surely. Or me. Would I go? I was baptized in the grace of God, because I asked the Reverend Birdsong about it and he said yes, I was. It's all down in the church book. If it was not down in the church book, I would be damned. Were you baptized in the grace of God, Gideon?"

"I think so," said Gideon.

"Was Pa?"

"Likely."

"Then that's not it," said Micah and got to his feet.

"What's not it?" Gideon gave the tether rope a pull and was satisfied with its holding. The calf would stay close to its mother, being too young to know it was free and thinking the whole world ended at its family's tail.

"Why you'll have the call. It wouldn't come from the Devil, as the Reverend Lapp says it does, unless you were damned, but you can't be damned if you're in the church book. Can you, Gideon?"

"Micah, I wish you'd not listen to the Reverend Lapp."

"I must. He talks so often. Gideon, may I go to the Ladies' Meeting? They'll be needing help with the pansies, most likely."

"No need to ask me where you can go and where you can't," Gideon said, almost sharply. "When I'm not here to answer, you'll be choosing for yourself."

Micah gazed at him for a moment, then shook the future out of his head and sprang away.

The journey to the village was the prettiest way in the world, cherry trees shaking out their snow and the sky all blue with only one cloud in it and a high-flying swift to promise a clear tomorrow.

It seemed to be a day when all the animals were playing. Rabbits wore their fur ruffled from leaping about in hedges, Mrs. Clegg's cock crowed in perfect recollection of dawn, and Mr. Lunny's little dog was down by the Meander, trying to catch the river with its own wet nose. Micah tricked a tadpole into his hands and let the dog sniff it, but the tadpole slipperied away and the dog trotted off, tail high, to find other rivers and chase them out from their banks.

Micah pranced up the high street as if it was laid with springy willow, bowed very polite to Miss Maidy and Miss Emma's front path, and then went round by the back door to stick his head through and say, "Dorrie."

There was a good deal of excitement in the kitchen, and Micah stopped on the threshold to admire it.

First, there was the table spread with all manner of little bakings: lacy tarts with pricked tops that bubbled, fat cakes crisscrossed with sticky runlets of jam, two fair round loaves, shiny-topped, one saffron yellow where the knife had made its first cut.

Then, there was the stove, glowing companionably, its bowed front bulging with more good smells escaping through the crack of the oven door. On its broad shiny top, the teakettle whistled like a blackbird, trying to hold its lid over the excited puffs of steam.

Then, there were the cats, Puss and the young lame one, Puss calm on the shelf, paws wrapped, deep round purr shaking his furry sides. The lame one stalked the kitchen, stiff-legged and chancy, skittering sideways like a blown leaf at the sound of the kettle, at the sight of Dorrie's shoes hurrying so fast across the scrubbed floor.

And, then, last and best, there was Dorrie herself, hair in a braid down her back, a big white apron muffling her gray woolen dress, sleeves rolled high and a streak of flour across her cheek. Micah stood and sniffed the kitchen and eyed the cats and appreciated Dorrie for almost a whole minute, and then he darted inside and seized the high stool to sit upon. The lame cat leaped onto his lap and Puss mewed and the teakettle's lid jumped and slid down over its long copper nose.

"Watch out with your fingers," said Dorrie, accepting him as she would a rain shower coming at a sudden moment. "These are hot." She slid a tray of snaps out of the oven, fruity and dark, and such a cloud of spices and currants and plumminess rose to the roof that Micah nearly fell off the stool.

"I've come to help," said Micah. "We tethered the cow, Gideon and me, and I came by the river with Mister Lunny's dog. Would you like me to fetch for you? Are the ladies here?"

She gave him a snap so hot it took his breath away, and in the space of silence she told him that the ladies had been sewing already for upwards of an hour and that, yes, he could fetch if he would be careful of the parlor.

"All the little slippy things on the tables," said Micah. "I know. And the ladies' dresses to fall over and their sewing silks and the fine cups. I can manage all that, Dorrie, except the fine cups. You'll take those in, and the teapot."

"Gideon's well?" said Dorrie, picking up the excited teakettle to pour water on the tea leaves and distracting Micah's nose with yet another cloud of fragrance.

"Will they eat all those cakes and things, Dorrie?" he said anxiously. "Here's one is burned."

"It is not burned," said Dorrie indignantly. "It's just the sugar that ran over."

"I know," Micah agreed, "but Gideon said I'm not to ask for cakes."

She gave it to him and spread a white cloth on the tray that was painted with roses and violets, arranging her bakings in tidy rows. Then she poured off the tea into a blue teapot and put a whole family of cups, as thin and white as eggshells, onto a smaller tray.

"The hen-cozy is still lost," said Dorrie worriedly. "Mrs Lapp will speak of it, and Miss Maidy will be flustered." She poured milk into a fat jug, and Puss made a noise in his throat toward the lame cat. The lame cat came running and twined begging paws around Dorrie's ankle, but it was a bad time to be making suggestions and, after a while, it went and sat under the table and Puss came down and lectured it.

"What hen-cozy?" said Micah.

"The one Mrs. Lapp made and Miss Maidy lost," said Dorrie, explaining everything. She sighed and picked up the tray of cups and teapot, smiled to reassure Micah that all would yet be well about the hen-cozy, and left the kitchen. Micah thought the matter over, then followed her with the big tray, bearing it into the parlor with a careful eye on his feet. He offered first choice of all the delicate things to Miss Maidy, which seemed only fitting in case Mrs. Lapp had started already to talk about the hen-cozy. Miss Maidy gave him a vague, pleased smile and took off her thimble so as not to bruise the little cakes.

Dorrie set the tea tray down in front of Miss Emma on a narrow-legged table with wood as dark and glimmery as the Meander at night. Mrs. Lapp sat up very straight and bit off a piece of purple thread. "I see you don't use the hen-cozy, Emma," said Mrs. Lapp.

Miss Emma pressed her lips together, Miss Maidy put her thimble back on as if she might hide in it, Dorrie looked down at the carpet.

"Puss's doing," said Micah, speaking loud. " 'Twas all lying ready on the table, the cozy was, and Puss took it. 'Twas terrible dirty before I got it back, being chased about all over the garden. You'd not have it here dirty?" he asked courteously.

"Oh," said Mrs. Lapp and sniffed. After a moment, she accepted a cherry tart, last summer's berries picked just ahead of the provoked birds.

"I've things in the oven," Dorrie said hurriedly, being partial to Miss Maidy as well as to the truth and not seeing at the moment how she could accommodate both.

Micah circled the tray placidly among the ladies. There was Mrs. Likewise, stout and square and a peril to her buttons; Mrs. Chessy, pale and fretting; Mrs. Lunny, who had forgotten her bodkin but scarcely liked to send for it from the tavern; Miss Oakley with a bonnet full of flowers and a cast in one eye; Mrs. Clegg, sparrow-like as ever and very neat with her toes on a footstool and her fingers taking tiny stitches in something long and black; Mrs. Cowhedge and her two daughters, looking more like rainspouts than ladies in their gusty brown dresses; and even Miss Preeb from the bakery who seldom came, being given to fits of giddiness but gay as a May-bug between times.

Mrs. Lapp sipped her tea with her finger crooked and finally, sighing heavily, addressed herself to Micah. "I hope," she said, "that you have been praying for your poor brother's soul."

All the ladies straightened their backs, except Miss Preeb who had dropped a fruit snap on the floor and was searching for it with noisy secrecy.

"It's kind in you to ask," said Micah affably.

"He'll be going soon, no doubt," Mrs. Lapp said. "In June, perhaps." She added, "The Devil has great powers then," possibly remembering all the courting and bewitchment of Midsummer Eve and the false foxglove on the hillsides. "Your father went in June."

"Put the tray down, Micah," said Miss Emma anxiously.

Micah put the tray down. June followed May. There was no

stopping the wild roses and the honeysuckle, the wasps and the haymaking and the meadowsweet. Gideon's going, which had been forever away, was scarcely tomorrow. He stared at them all.

"Really, Amelia—"

Micah ignored her. "*Where* is the Devil?" he said passionately. "Where is he about? Where do I find him?"

"The Devil," said Mrs. Lapp possessively, "is everywhere. If your mother ever saw fit to send you to the Sabbath sermons, you would not need to ask. My son has told from the pulpit where the Devil is. This is a sinful village." She thrust her needle into the heart of a purple pansy and thought with bitterness of the Reverend Birdsong who refused to admit it was sinful at all.

"Amelia!" said Mrs. Likewise, rising and scattering pins all over the roses on the carpet.

"You'll not deny, Aggie," said Mrs. Lapp, fixing her with a hard eye, "that when the Devil had his hold on Mr. Clegg, it was my son who saved him." She bowed to Mrs. Clegg.

Mrs. Clegg said, "Oh, yes, indeed," and burst into tears from the excitement.

There was such a flurry and rising of ladies that the air seemed to be full of needles and swing silks and little cakes. Miss Maidy, chirping tenderly, went to pat Mrs. Clegg.

"I think we need more tea," said Miss Emma calmly. "Amelia, do sit down and talk less. Micah is not—Where *is* the child?"

They looked, searching about as if he might be inside a packet of pins, but he was not to be found. When they called Dorrie, she only knew that he had passed through the kitchen, taking two tea cakes and a hot snap with him and had not said where he was going.

The taking of the sweets reassured them all, and they found their thimbles and clicked them and settled again in their circle, fussing gently. Mrs. Lapp sniffed and handed one end of the pansy cloth to Aggie Likewise who eyed it mistrustfully for a moment, then took it and began to stitch a purple petal as if it was a burdock spike.

"He was in a hurry," said Dorrie and went back to the kitchen.

"It turns dark early," Mrs. Lapp said defensively. "Little boys should be home by dark."

"Really, Amelia!" said Miss Emma, and handed her a cup of cold, unsugared tea.

*CHAPTER SEVENTEEN*

T HERE WERE three likely places for the Devil to be found.

There was the Meander at the spot where the long-ago pastor had drowned, marked for years by a cloven hoof-print in the riverbank which had finally washed away in the full floods.

There was the well that the boggle had fallen into. Boggles were near kin to the Devil, and, even though this boggle had long since clambered out, there was always a mist over the well at moon-up and no telling who stood tall in the mist.

And, last of all, there were the woods, not the woods that were young and stood in an astonishment of green about the meadows, but the great old woods where nobody went at night except the owls.

He would try the river first, then the boggle's well, and perhaps he would not have to go to the woods at all. What to say or do when he found the Devil, Micah did not know, but perhaps it would all come clear in his mind like the tale of Puss and the hen-cozy. And, like the hen-cozy, all would suddenly be well, and he could go triumphant home with the news that

Gideon, like the cow, might stay forever.

The sun was not quite down and the gold of its light came through the willows and caught them in a shower of green rain. A thrush sang from a bough as if it thought morning was about, and there was a splash as an otter slipped sleekly from the bank and into the stream, the water in a travel behind it.

It was easy to find the place where the river had sighed itself together over the pastor's drowning head, because the gray rock nearby had been split to mark the good man's passing with a cross driven in to give him hope of heaven.

Micah sat down on the rock and ate his snap, and twice in the dimming light he thought he saw the drowned pastor's hat afloat, but each time it was only an island of whirling sod. He watched the river turn black and the moon begin to climb, and still there was no sign of the Devil. He pulled his knees up under his chin and wound his arms about and gave himself up to thinking of Gideon's call.

It was not a told tale any longer, not since Mrs. Lapp spoke out. It was something that was real and would happen, likely in June. There would come a June day with the sun high, wild strawberries turning red and meadow-sweet as tangled as Sheby's hair. There would be long green shadows on the hillsides, grasshoppers fidgeting the meadow, yellow flags by the Meander. And there would be nothing so different about Gideon walking down the road, except that he would not come back.

The calf would turn into a cow. The baby coming to the cradle would learn to walk. The sun would rise with no one to sit by Micah on the cow shed roof, and the pig would not like his corn so well from someone else's hand. There would be fewer in the bed and lonesomer, and no Gideon to speak to about the troubles that sometimes came.

The three hens and a cock that Gideon talked of would never matter any more, with Gideon wandering. In Indy and China, they would not have hens surely and no place for a broody nest. They had been going to have a broody nest in the shed, Gideon had promised it.

There must be some way to hold back the call from its thieving. If the Devil would only come—

Micah closed his eyes and wished very long and hard, but when he opened them again there was only the moon still climbing and the river going along as it had before, lisp and scold. Around him in the night, all the small things purred and clucked, and once a glowworm danced.

He sighed and ate a tea cake, very lingeringly, then sat for a while licking sugar off his fingers. Finally, he leaned from the rock and put his face down close to the water, staring into it with his two eyes staring back. The water was not roiled at all, not even a little. Perhaps the drowned pastor had settled into peace at last.

"It's the cross!" said Micah suddenly. "The Devil would not be coming here when there's a cross in the rock. I'm no more than a gawk not to have been thinking of that, and all this time's gone by." Complaining of himself, he pushed his leaf tea cake back into his pocket, since there might be a long wait at the boggle's well, and started toward the hill and the winding path as fast as if the well might flee before his coming.

He went by the long road and not by the Clegg farm because the boy Tattery, who felt the moon in his bones, might be up and around, and this was a private search. The path to the well was as silver as the night, the weeds silver and the pebbles that rolled under Micah's toes, and the blackberry tangle. The mist over the well-hole came on him suddenly, rising straight like chimney smoke on a still day, and through the mist there showed the glimmer of a cherry tree with tiny silvered leaves.

Micah went up to the well confidently, being used to it, and blew with puffed cheeks at the mist, which wavered and turned to gray rags and then came softly together again. There was nobody and nothing in the middle of it, but he had known that already or he would not have been able to see the cherry tree.

He kneeled and put his mouth to the well-hole and spoke very clearly into it. An echo rode up on a cold blade rush of air and brushed his skin and went on past him, but that had happened before and it was not the boggle. He squatted on his heels thoughtfully and looked about him. There was a thornbush close by, which was hopeful because all the familiars of the night were well known to be partial to thornbushes, stitching black garments with long black needles.

Also, it was here that the Devil had last been seen in Greenwillow, Mr. Proudfoot tumbling backward in a frothing fit. Afterwards all was quiet for many years until the Reverend Lapp had come with his special visions. Then the Devil had turned busy, shaking the pulpit about, traveling with little Fox Jones and, finally, losing a terrible battle against the Angel of the Lord alongside Mr. Clegg's deathbed.

Micah, recollecting this last, gave a wail of aggravation, fiercer even than he had felt by the river, and a wakeful rabbit leaped in the thornbush. "He'd not be here either," said Micah, outraged, to the night. "He'd not be staying so near where the angel came."

It did seem that the crosses and angels about were making it very hard to meet up with the Devil. Now there was nowhere to go but to the great woods.

After a moment's thinking, he ate his last tea cake, feeling it would give him comfort inside. This must have been so because, as he walked across the meadow and down the steep hill and along the wide road, he walked very light. The dewfall was cold on his toes, and the moon pulled him up by his hair, so it was for all as if he was skimming the silver earth. The more he floated, the more sure he felt that the Devil was going to be easy to have dealing with, and Gideon would never have to go wandering.

A whippoorwill spoke out of a clump of leaves caught high in a tree under the moon, and Micah whistled an answer and carried the tune with him right to the edge of the great woods.

He stepped in, lightfooted, and they closed about him.

The moon did not leave him, but it changed. Instead of a great silver lantern showing everything clear—rut in the road and thorn on the bush, rabbit's tail and tea-cake crumbs and white mist rising above the well—it turned itself into long silver fingers, reaching down through scare-crow bushes, black massed leaves holding the sky away.

Micah stopped and peered about him and wished that Sheby were by so that he could hold her hand and teach her not to be frightened, here in the great woods late on a May night. They had come together and often, but always by daylight when there were paths that could be followed, pulling winter ivy from under snow or looking for the fat moss cushions with yellow pintips to dry for fire clods.

No paths showed now, only roots that lay clawing at the ground. Micah slid silently from one tree to the next, the moon's fingers following him. A bat clapped leather wings and an owl hooted, and the earth was all cold-leafed wetness. He thought of turning back but then he thought of June without

Gideon, and all the months that would come after June.

Perhaps by luck he might find a witch's knuckle-ring, the woven circle of dry grass with no beginning and no end that the witches wore on wind-nights and sometimes dropped in the great woods. There was much power in a witch's knuckle-ring, though no one knew just what kind, and perhaps a witch's power would help in dealings with the Devil.

"Even by light there's no finding the rings," said Micah a little mournfully, and he heard his voice go past him on either side, whispering. His toes curled and he wished he had worn shoes. But who would think to wear shoes to the Ladies' Meeting in May? He listened for the whippoorwill's noise, hoping the bird would call and say he was not alone, but the only sound was a wind that crept about very high in the dark branches, moving under the moon.

The woods were beginning to come closer. Fingers and fists reached down from the trees, and once he ducked a dangling, hanged branch, and something chuckled. "I'm not feared," said Micah firmly and wished he knew how to say the Lord's Prayer backwards as a charm against evil, until he remembered it was Evil itself that he was hunting for. He tried whistling but a long-past crumb of tea cake must have stuck in his throat and the best he could manage was a reedy call, very sad in the dark.

"Is someone about?" said Micah finally, speaking very loud. He could hear the woods listening and, when a twig cracked under his foot, they all jumped, together, the trees rasping their long fingers and murmuring. He thought determinedly of Ma and Gideon and the cow and how glad all would be when he returned home with the news that he had persuaded the Devil, but there was no sign at all of flames or thunder in these cold black woods, only the sick white moon and the twisted trees.

Perhaps another time would be altogether wiser. He would come back with his shoes on, shoes and a shawl for his nose which was getting as cold as the moonlight. Also a packet of food for the hollow in his middle. He remembered that there had been a soup kettle on the back of the stove all day, with a marrowbone very juicy in it, and he thought of it wishfully, tasting it salt on his tongue and simmering hot from the kettle.

He should be going home. Ma and Gramma and all would be wondering where he had got off to, and Jabez would steal his share of the soup. Likely the Devil was somewhere else altogether tonight, with his followers around him. Likely the full moon troubled the Devil, lighting too much the edge of the darkness he carried about.

Perhaps after all the Reverend Lapp should have been consulted with, before coming to the woods. Micah looked ahead and to each side of him and saw only shadow on shadow going away forever, and then he turned his head and looked backward over his shoulder.

High in a tree, something cried.

"Owl," said Micah rapidly, trying not to notice the ice in his bones. "Flying about in the moon," said Micah, "coming out of his nest to look at me. I shall tell Sheby how the owl came out of his nest—" He turned slowly about in a circle, his eyes darting, his ears pricked to the scantiest rustling. The tree cried again, high up.

Micah said, "I shall go home. There's the soup to eat and Sheby to tell and no one's about tonight. Woods are very quiet and it's cold for May. All frozen over." He touched his hand to his nose and, though it was reassuringly there, it felt frozen too. "I shall go home" he said again, and started to push through the trees. They had been edging closer while he stood thinking, and he had not expected this.

The broken tree in front of him when he turned had not been there before. He must have come into the woods from the other side, so he turned about again, and there was a bush, very mean and scraggy, scraping its twigs about though there was no wind.

Micah turned once more, very carefully in a quarter-circle so he would not come to face either the broken tree or the scraggy bush, looking for something to show the way he had entered. Everything was strange.

He spun very quick, all the way about, like a cat chasing its tail, thinking to surprise the place he had lost, but it did no good. Broken tree, scraggy bush, two hooded tall trees, strange to his eye. Worse, the moon was slipping away, the bright along the branches feathering off. Nothing was white on black any longer, but only dark on dark.

For the third time, the tree cried out.

It was only an owl or a witch or the moon caught on a branch, but Micah's feet, cold on the cold ground, gave a great leap. They fled with him whether he wished or not, branches whipping across his path and twisty vines catching at his knees.

It seemed as if he ran forever, like a rabbit before a fox, blind in the dark and his breath hurting in his throat. Then, in the black, in the forest that was closing tighter and tighter around him, a tree root snatched and clutched its claws around his ankle. Head over foot, still fleeing, he tumbled into a tangle of bush.

He lay there, rolled to a ball like a hedgehog, listening and shaking. After a while he realized that the pounding and all the ragged sounds were inside himself. He laid his face against the ground, but there was a spell on him and the leaves grew wet under his cheek. Micah snuffled. "It's the misery," he said to himself inside his huddled ball. "I'm getting the misery like Gramma got." The thought of Gramma, all warm and asleep by the hearth, made the misery worse and he tried very hard to stop shaking but it was not at all easy.

"I'm lost," said Micah finally, and he curled tighter as if he would be less lost if he was smaller. His legs and his chest ached with running, but under the bush was quiet and nothing reached him.

After a while he began to feel warmer, rolled so tight, and the lids of his eyes got as heavy as water. The darkness was soft around him, and there was no sound of owls. His eyelids drooped, opened slowly, drooped.

When he opened them again, the Devil was coming.

He came as a bright light, a handful of flames moving through the darkness. Terror turned Micah's bones to water, and a tree called out his name quite clearly. "Micah!"

He shrank into the ground, ears closed, eyes closed, breath stopped off as if he would like to be dead like Mr. Clegg in his coffin where no one could find him. But the Devil's light pounced and pried open his eyes without their wanting. The light from hell swung in a slow circle, and the voice called.

Micah knew it at once. It was the voice that would call Gideon away on his wanderings, and the light that would show him the long path that led from home. And Gideon could not escape it.

Suddenly Micah cried out in defiance.

He forgot how great the Devil was and how fearful, and he remembered only Gideon and the awfulness of Gideon's going. Before his bones could huddle again or his heart pin him with its faintness to the ground, Micah leaped out of the bush and rushed through the darkness straight at the Evil One. Spinning and stumbling, Micah ran, forgetting reason and fear alike.

This was the true Satan, the one who turned the Reverend Lapp so white in the pulpit just to name his name. This was the Devil who stalked Greenwillow for its wickedness and took the earth up in his dark fingers and left all strangled. This was the Power that had taken Pa and would now take Gideon.

"No!" cried Micah, and went, without thinking, to do great battle.

He flung himself at the light, his fists pounding what stood behind it and his feet kicking and his voice screaming very loud so that he could not listen to his own terror. "You can't have him!" Micah shouted. "You can't have Gideon!"

"Praise be to God," said the Devil, and turned into the Reverend Birdsong.

Micah burst into tears.

The Reverend Birdsong lifted up his voice with some difficulty, having sustained Micah in his middle. "Gideon," he called. "Gideon, come here. I've found him. There, child, you're all right, we've found you."

Micah came out of the reverend's middle with both fists rubbing his eyes, and blinked rapidly to show he had not been crying. He looked at the Devil's lamp in the reverend's hand, and it was only the old lantern that hung on a hook by the doorway. It came over him very heavily how ill-behaved it was to mistake a reverend for the Evil One, and he eyed Mr. Birdsong with dismay.

Gideon came pushing through the underwood, thornbushes stepping out of his path. "Micah!" said Gideon in just the same voice that the reverend had used for praising God.

"I mistook him, Gideon," Micah said hastily. "I was upside

down in a spinney bush, and the light mazed me."

The Reverend Birdsong said, "Perfectly natural," in a thoughtful way. He then added, "Micah, what were you doing upside down in a spinney bush in the middle of the wood at half after midnight? If you don't mind my asking."

"I was seeking the Devil," said Micah, holding fast to Gideon. "Mrs. Lapp, she told me the Devil would call to Gideon in June, and I thought to talk to him. I went to the river and he was not there, and I went to the boggle's well and he was not there. So I came here."

Gideon and the Reverend Birdsong looked at each other far a long moment, and nothing moved but the lights of their two lanterns. Then Gideon said gently, "Micah, you're young to understand, but there's nothing could come of talk with the Devil. The call's not his doing, whatever the Reverend Lapp says or Mrs. Lapp either. It's a claim laid on our family, firstborn to firstborn."

Micah looked down at the ground, and the misery came back on him very strong.

Gideon said, "Listen to me, Micah. After I've gone, there's to be no others called. It all ends with my going. I promise you."

Birdsong looked at them both, shaking his head. Micah said slowly, "It'd not have helped then, even if I'd found the Devil? He's very great."

"There's those who are greater," said the reverend shortly. "Gideon, it's a long journey back and the child's wivvering like a flea. Eyes closed," said Mr. Birdsong severely, "and tongue still going."

"No such thing," said Micah and found himself swung to Gideon's shoulder like meal in a sack going to the pig. It came to him that the pig must have been missing him, gone so long, and Sheby too; most likely, and he thought of all there would be to tell. But then he thought how Gideon had said that even the Devil could not change matters and how June was no longer forever away in time, and a heavy sadness came on him. He sighed with his whole heart and fell suddenly asleep, there in the deep woods with Gideon's arms around him.

The light of the house shone ahead for them and Martha's shadow, great with the coming child, moved against it. Gideon spoke at last.

"He's such a young one," said Gideon, "and the call won't wait until he's grown."

The Reverend Birdsong shook himself all over, as if ridding himself of black trees and crying things.

"Seeking out the Devil in a dark wood," said Gideon wonderingly. "Thinking to help me, Micah was."

Birdsong said, "No need to be afraid for him, Gideon. When he thought I was the Devil, he ran toward me, not away."

"I'll not forget," said Gideon, and then he lifted up his voice and called out of the night. "Ma, he's found!"

# CHAPTER EIGHTEEN

GRAMMA SAT in her chair out under the oldest tree, dandelions so thick around her that the high June grass turned butter yellow where the rockers seesawed. As she rocked, she hummed, a mizzy droning hard to tell from the sound of the brown bees.

She was having a feast of tiny sun-hot wild strawberries, poking them out one by one from their basket and glancing around quick before each swallow. The strawberries belonged to Shadrach and Obadiah, but they ought to have known better than to trust her with them and this thought relieved Gramma of any sense of sinfulness. She rocked and hummed and tasted, sunshine on her cranky bones and her thieving fingers.

Martha came out the door with the milk pail in her hand and bent with difficulty to put it down by the step, where it could fill itself with the air that smelled of clover and strawberries.

"A few more sun-ups and y'r apron strings won't tie," said Gramma, speaking through a mouthful. "Y'r time is sure mighty close."

Martha sighed and leaned in the doorway, looking up at high clouds and the everlasting sky. "Seems forever this time,

193

ma. And it won't lay still."

"Roistering around," said Gramma, "and a-hittin' its end on the ceiling. Must be a girl in there. Whyn't you set down?"

"I'm easier standing. Sheby'd be real pleased with a sister, but Amos he said he'd planted a boy and we was to call it Jeremiah."

"Jeremiah was a woeful man," said Gramma. "What'll you call a girl? They was a Jezebel in the Holy Book, that's real close-sounding to Jeremiah."

"Jezebel's pretty," said Martha and tried the name out four times like a charm-song. "We c'd call her Jessy for her little name, like Sheby for Bathsheba." She closed her eyes for a moment against the shimmer of sun and the dancing grass.

"Real hot, 'tis," said Gramma, curling her toes and scowling upwards at a mockingbird picking its notes out of the green leaves. "Cat-cally things, never could abide 'em." She said sharply, "Near Midsummer, ain't it?"

"Nigh on," said Martha. "Sheby and Obadiah and Shadrach, they'll be gathering fernseed real soon now. Jabez says he don't want to turn invisible, and Micah ain't got the time. Might be nice, ma," she said. "Maybe I'll try this year."

Gramma cackled. "Take a lot more'n fernseed to vanish you, girl. 'F you don't have that young un pretty soon now, you won't git through the door."

"They oughta be some easier way of bringin' babies," Martha said. "All this waitin' around and gettin' as big as a cow—"

"Anyways it starts good," said Gramma and cackled again like a rowdy hen. Then she leaned forward, peering. "Ain't that Dorrie a-coming?"

Martha moved her shoulders away from the door and set

the load of her coming child even on her feet again. "Now that's real nice," she said warmly, and lifted up her voice in a welcoming "Dorrie!"

Dorrie came running light across the summer ground, and Gramma's eyes flew to the basket on her arm. "Cakes," said Gramma greedily.

"Pie," said Dorrie. "Early-cherry pie. I'd have culled them redder, but the birds were thicker than the berries and Miss Emma likes them sharp." She held the pie out toward Martha, a little shyly as if it would be kind in her to accept it.

Martha said, "It's beautiful, Dorrie, all fancy around the edge. I'd never have the patience."

"Should I put it in the cupboard where it's out of reach?" said Dorrie. "I'll put it high."

"There's nothing that's out of Jabez's reach."

"I know." Dorrie went to the house, carrying the pie carefully, and the white geese came waddling in hope of yellow corn and followed her over the threshold, siffling and pecking. Dorrie shushed them and then stood, quite still and dismayed, and looked about her.

It was never a tidy place, the Briggses' house, not like her home kitchen with the pans all shiny and the big stove and the scrubbed floor. But she had never seen it looking like it did now, all clutter and happenstance, shoes in the hearthplace, kettle all grimy, cats on the biggest bed, and a drabble-tailed quilt on the floor. Dorrie ran to put the pie in the cupboard and, there on the shelf, was a huge spider staring out at her from its spider house.

From the doorway, Martha said, "Tisn't usually such a muddle, Dorrie. Seems like every time I try to lean, the baby kicks. Sheby means to help but she's jumpier than the baby even.

Mostly I don't fret, but just lately—" She sat heavily on a chair, her hands loose in her lap, and looked up at Dorrie. "I'll be glad when this little un's born, Dorrie, and that's a fact."

Dorrie smoothed her skirt and looked down at the floor, which she always did when she had a favor to ask, and finally she managed to say it. "Could I scrub just a little? I'd put all back where I found it."

Martha started to say it wasn't fitting for Dorrie to be doing her work, but Dorrie paid her no mind. She had her eye on the scouring-stone and the broom behind the door, and in a minute the quilt was billowing and the dust was scuttling and the cats were standing about as vexed as if there was thunder in the sky. Dorrie, lost in the middle of it all, started to sing like the first thrush in the morning, it being June and a broom in her hand and Gideon's house.

Martha went out the door, and a moment later a cloud of bright dust, catching sunshine, flew after her, provoking the geese. Gramma sneezed with imagination and yelled to Dorrie that she was like to choke. Martha said, "Hush, ma. It's real kind of her."

"Huh," said Gramma, "she relishes it. 'F you put Dorrie into a rabbit hole, she'd set up house. Nesty as a wren, Dorrie is, oughta be settin' on her own eggs right now. Gideon's a fool. With all I've done for him, he still ain't got no more sense than a pea pod." She rocked a minute, thought a minute and added, "I could eat a bit of pie now, it'd tempt my appetite mebbe. I'm failing, I'm failing fast. Don't hardly eat at all no more. Girl!"

But Martha had her eyes closed, listening to June, and Gramma made a huffy sound. From the house there came a clatter of pots, and a cat leaped through the window. "Besoming about," said Gramma, "allus straightenin' and stirrin' and scrubbin'. It ain't healthy. But she's agreeable, Dorrie is, and cherry pies don't hang on bushes. He's a fool, that Gideon," said Gramma sternly and went to sleep.

Down in the meadow, "Who's singing?" said Micah, standing still with an armful of grass and a load of blossoms, ready to spread and dry in the sun. The cow who had been watching with calm eyes while they reaped her meadow, raised her head and her bell jingled. The calf came to make sure of her and nudged her flank, and Gideon put down the scythe he was making sharp with a honing stone and reached out his hand to the little animal.

"Likely Ma or Sheby," said Gideon, thinking it might be Dorrie.

"Might be Dorrie," said Micah.

"Might be." Gideon dropped his hand with the fingers up, making a cup of it, and the soft calf nose thrust and nuzzled. "Micah, come autumn, the calf'll be weaning. You'll teach it to drink."

Micah laid his bundle down and a butterfly drifted onto it, delicate as the air, pale-blue wings opening and closing as soft as breath. "Gideon," said Micah, "could Sheby wean the calf?"

"Sheby?" said Gideon, startled.

"It's come to me," Micah said, "that I could travel with you when you get your call. You'll be going to places very far off with no one to talk to, it'll seem very quiet. Ma's got Gramma, Sheby's got Ma, everybody's got somebody to talk to. I'd not be missed." He looked at Gideon for a long moment, then shook his head. "No, you'd not let me."

"You're needed, Micah," Gideon said. He stroked the little calf with his fingers and she liked it for a moment and then galloped off, gay and awkward. "I'll come home, times."

"Will you stay then, or will you go away as soon as you've come, like Pa?"

"I can't tell," Gideon said slowly. "I'll not make a promise, Micah, and then hurt you with not keeping it. It's burden enough on you that I have to go." He straightened his shoulders and nodded at the rakings. "Anyways, I know the meadow'll not wait," he said and swung the scythe in a long arc that caught sunshine on its blade and plunged deep into the grass.

Micah leaned to scoop a double armful of greenness and bloom, and then spoke upside down with his head in clover and daisies. "Shall I hear it when it calls you? Is it like thunder, Gideon, or is it very thin and far away off in the world? Shall I be hearing it, do you think? Sometimes at night I think I do, since I came back from hunting the Devil. The Reverend Birdsong, he says you were right about the Devil, that he'd have paid me no heed. . . . Gideon, Mister Lapp did get the Angel of the Lord to come and wait on Mister Clegg's soul. Mightn't he—"

"Micah," said Gideon, "be quiet." Then he put down his scythe and pulled Micah to him, armful of meadow and all, and Micah leaned his nose somewhere in the middle of Gideon's shirt and gave a very small snuffle. "We're brothers of each other," said Gideon. "Our ma was different, but we're brothers still. Micah, you know if there was any choice, I'd never be going. You've had the telling of that a hundred times."

Micah backed out. "You might be mistook," he said passionately, "you might go too soon. How do you know when it's the call a-coming? It might be a wood dove very lonesome. It might be the Meander with the rain a-coming down. How can you tell if it's not owls?"

"There's no mistaking," Gideon said, and wished he could find the words that would make Micah stop his hoping. He leaned and pulled a strangleweed from out of the ground, and it brought earth up with it, warm to the touch and full of promising. He'd dreamed once of having a wheat meadow, gold as a sunset with the wind running across it, like he'd dreamed of three hens and a cock.

He let the dirt crumble warm and soft in his fingers for a moment longer, and then he gave the strangleweed a shake, loosing the last hold of the snarled roots, and threw it away from him.

There would be no mistaking the call when it came, he knew that. If it came this moment—the meadow not gleaned and the baby not born—he would have to go where it led him, down the road and along the river, till river ran into river and bay at last and ocean at last.

And, after the ocean, no knowing what. Only that it would be a long time before he felt the brown earth of his own land again, lying gentle in his fingers.

"That's Dorrie that's singing," said Micah, suddenly and very positively. "Likely she's brought us a pie. Do you think—"

He half turned toward the song, knowing that if he followed it he would find something. If not a pie, a small cake or a fat hot sugar-bun.

Then, "Meadow's to be gathered," said Micah solidly, and bent to his task.

#  CHAPTER NINETEEN

I N THE sleeping house, Puss was the first to hear the pounding on the door.

Early in the evening the brindled cat had been made very fretful at a mousehole behind the woodbox, out of which nothing came at all but a suggestion of whiskers. Then he had been plagued by the lame young cat, wanting to play and flying about through the air with scattered paws and mild eyes. And, finally, the parlor windowsill (the best sleeping-haunt of a June night) had been taken over by wild pink roses, an offering from the Reverend Birdsong.

The roses were meant for Aggie Likewise but she would have none of them, declaring they brought ill fortune and wasps. Mr. Birdsong had come at once to Miss Maidy, apologizing for the roses' wickedness, and she had given them shelter without any respect for Puss's habits.

Puss, finding himself ousted, stalked the house, grumbling and muttering, then settled in a heap on the parlor carpet, ears, paws, nose and tail folded into the after-bedtime dark. When the racketing at the door roused him, he sprang into the air, spitting, and flighted up the stairs to find Miss Maidy.

She was coming out of her room with a candle in her hand and her face very anxious under the sleeping cap's frill. "Dear, dear," said Miss Maidy, clutching at the trail of her nightdress, "who can it be at this hour, so near Midsummer Eve too? No knowing what's about. Emma—Emma, love!"

Miss Emma emerged with a shawl around her head and said to get Dorrie, and Dorrie appeared as if their need had brought her rather than the noise. "I'll see who it is," said Dorrie bravely and, shielding her candle with one hand, she ran down the stairs, pulled back the latch and threw the door open to whatever waited.

It was Sheby, frantic on the doorstep. "Dorrie, it's Ma," she said, tumbling her words out. "She wants you should come, and Gramma wants you should, too. She's skeered, Gramma is."

"The baby, Sheby—it's come?"

"Baby's been coming since moon-up. Ma started the pains and Gramma, she said the baby'd pop out quicker'n spit, you know like the little calf come. But, Dorrie, that was so many hours ago and there's nothing happened yet." She gave a little wail of fright. " 'Cept Ma, it hurts her."

"I'll come, Sheby, quick as I can make ready." Dorrie looked at Sheby for a moment, then said, "Will you wait, or will you go back?"

"I'm to fetch Mrs. Hasty," said Sheby, remembering. "Gramma said we need her, though she's not been needed before, not ever. She's so monstrous big, Mrs. Hasty is, that Mister Hasty'll have to hitch up the horse and bring her in the wagon, that's trouble enough, and then—"

"Hurry, Sheby," said Dorrie gently and turned her around, stopping the runaway of words that Sheby could not stop herself. "I'll go straight to your ma. Run fast, and try not to be fearing."

"We'll pray for you," said Miss Maidy suddenly, and watched as Sheby leaped away into the darkness, sniffling a little because she was scared but running like a deer.

"I'll put some things in a basket," said Miss Emma firmly and went to the kitchen. Dorrie ran to dress. Miss Maidy bent down and picked Puss up, holding his large furriness very tight against her, and for once he made no objection. After a moment she put him down and went to get Dorrie's blue cloak from the peg.

Basket and cloak were to hand, along with Miss Maidy and Miss Emma, when in no more than in a cat-wink of time Dorrie slipped down the stairs. "The lantern," Miss Maidy said anxiously. "Dorrie must have the lantern. There's no moon."

"It's lit already and set out by the kitchen step," Miss Emma said. "I wish our bones were younger, Dorrie. Stay as long as you're needed, and don't fret your head about us."

"No, don't fret whatever you do," said Miss Maidy, echoing, but she said it to the night. Dorrie was gone already, a glow of lantern light running down the path and through the gate and out onto the dark road.

"Dear, the poor little ones," said Miss Maidy. "Emma love, shouldn't we tell the reverends?"

"Yes," Miss Emma said, "I suppose we should."

Nobody stirred in Greenwillow as Dorrie hurried down the road, basket on arm and lantern swinging its daffodil light. If there were cats about at Mrs. Likewise's, they kept to their shadowy ways and not even a bird peeped in the scented dark. Outside the tavern, Mr. Lunny's little dog twitched in his sleep as Dorrie's light footsteps hurried by, but his dreams stayed in their neat packet and were all of the soupbone he had buried in Miss Oakley's verbena bed.

The church slept, pews and hymnbooks and unswung bell, and even the owls in the bell tower drowsed in the warm night. Dorrie signed the air as she passed the steepled shadow, breathed a prayer and hurried along the river.

In all the night, only the Meander was still awake, lamentation among the reeds, stammer and plash where a rock broke its surface, but most of the time a clear running song like a long ballading.

It seemed lonesome for a moment when she left the river's company and turned westerly, but the pale flowers had taken the grass and there was more starshine in the meadow than there was in the sky. The walking was so easy to the foot that Dorrie thought to blow her lantern out, but then she remembered that a light seen coming might be a comfort to those who were waiting. Her heart ran ahead and her feet hurried to catch up, and it was only a quickness in time before she heard Gideon's voice and saw him moving through the dark toward her.

He took the lantern out of her hand and said, "Dorrie, it's you."

His voice was so troubled she wanted terribly to stay and comfort him, but she was needed indoors. "Sheby's gone to rouse Mrs. Hasty," Dorrie said and ran past him, past Jabez bedded and asleep under the big tree with his arm around Rip's neck, and past Shadrach and Obadiah sitting up and bravely keeping their eyes open in case they were wanted. A voice out of the darkness said explainingly, "Dorrie's come. All's all right now." Dorrie said, "I'm come, Micah," and went on into the house.

Martha was lying on the big bed with a twisted blanket across her and Gramma leaning over, crooning and scolding,

"Lie easy, dearie, there, lie easy. There's help a-coming." She heard the door and turned. "It's Dorrie," she said crossly. "Better a hundred years late than not at all. I s'pose. Never mind me, I'm just like to die with the worryin', that's all, but who cares about old Gramma? There, dearie, there, love."

Dorrie undid the clasp of her blue cloak and dropped it to the floor. She came to the bed and kneeled down and took Martha's hands in her own, finding them held so tight it hurt. But when Martha spoke, her voice sounded like it always did, only a little hoarse. "Did Sheby go for Mrs. Hasty?"

Dorrie nodded. "Are the pains bad?"

"Not so bad now. When they first come, I thought sure the baby'd be out and bouncing on the floor afore I got to the bed, but now it seems like it's turned ornery . . . . Dorrie, is it late?"

"Close on to sunrise," said Dorrie.

"Birthin' things allus like to come at sunrise," Martha said hopefully.

"Even the calf," said Dorrie, leaning over close to shut out everything but the thought of dawn and of little things getting born.

"Where's Sheby?"

"Gone for Mrs. Hasty."

Martha turned her head on the pillow. "I forgot. I asked you that already. We sent her because she runs so fast, faster than Micah even. Are the young uns all right, Dorrie?"

"They're waiting outside, and Gideon's taking care. Would you like a sip of water or some broth maybe?"

"Pain's let loose for a moment," Martha said. "Better leave me lay quiet. It's good Gideon ain't had his call yet."

"Yes, it's good." Dorrie turned her head at the sound of harness-jingle, listening.

Gideon came in at the door. "Mrs. Hasty's come," he began, then stopped, seeing how white Martha lay on the pillow, her hair tumbled and damp about her forehead, and her face somehow swollen and strange-looking. "Are you hurting Ma?" he asked.

" 'Tain't so bad, Gideon," said Martha.

Dorrie freed one hand gently and wiped the sweat from Martha's forehead with a corner of the blanket. "Gideon, don't stay," she said softly.

He looked at them both for a long moment. "Pa ought to be here," he said angrily. "He ought never have taken a wife," and then he turned and went out the door.

Over her shoulder Dorrie saw him go and in that small space of time, between footstep and closing door, all the hope she had that Gideon might wed her went away. His voice had told her all the things that could not be said against his father, the wandering man who had left a child not borned behind him.

For just a moment Dorrie kept her head turned away, feeling the love she had for Gideon ache all through her and seeing how it would run begging all her life long. Then she turned back. She couldn't do anything about the loving which would be with her forever, and Martha mustn't see her cry.

"There, love," she said tenderly, using the words Martha used herself when a child fell or sobbed or lost a treasure.

A great gusty sigh swelled from the doorway, and Mrs. Hasty, a vast pudding of a woman, wide as the Meander where it stretched in swampland, lumbered into the house, shaking out a large white apron as she came. She looked at Martha, clicked her tongue, then at Gramma and Dorrie. "Just the one of you to stay," she said. "You, girl."

"I'm stayin'," said Gramma with spirit.

"They ain't room," said Mrs. Hasty. "If I turn round, you'll be squoze into the wall and die suffocatin'."

"My own son's lawful wedded wife," said Gramma, "and you tell me to go outside. Brought all the other uns into the world, I did, without a lick o' help. Now I'm no more good to nobody 'n a mess of beans. Be better off dead and buried in my narrer grave." She looked at Mrs. Hasty sharply. "Mind you take good care o' her. Them pains started before the moon come up."

"I know," said Mrs. Hasty, turning her basket upside down all over the floor to find what she wanted in it. "Sheby talked all the way ridin' up, poor little midgins. You get outside to Sheby and the other uns, they're needin' you. We'll get this baby birthed atween us, if the Lord's willing."

"Amen," said Gramma and scuffed her way outside where she settled her shaky bones on the step, ear listening at the door crack and eye on the young ones while she waited for the dawn.

It seemed to be lost somewhere, up in the hills beyond the Meander, so slow it came. At last the darkness grayed, and out of it trees crept and the shape of the house. The geese came, stepping and pecking, and Gideon from milking with the pail in his hands and Micah close at his heels.

The lamplight indoors grew paler and paler as the gray light reached across the land, touching grass and flower head, chimney smoke and roof, Jabez's sleeping and the fur of Rip's ruff. Down on the Clegg farm, the cock crowed. A bird sang three bright pure notes and then hushed.

The Reverend Lapp and the Reverend Birdsong, coming as fast as they could, heard the sweet short song and looked at each other. "A lost soul," said Mr. Lapp promptly, seeing the innocent morning as if it lay under a blight of frost. "The child's, unshriven! We are too late."

"If you mean the baby," said Birdsong, who was having trouble keeping up and greatly out of breath, "it's very likely not even born yet. And if it is born, that's no reason why it should be dead. And if it *is* dead, it's not damned, Lapp, I won't have it."

"There is a curse on Amos Briggs's family," said the Reverend Lapp.

"Oh, nonsense." Birdsong tripped over a sprawl of blackberry vine, which had certainly not been in Lapp's path a moment earlier. "Oh, dear, dear. I beg your pardon."

"Granted," said Lapp icily.

"Not yours," said Birdsong.

Lapp looked back over his shoulder and reminded himself that one must bear one's cross. "I warned Gideon," he said, "but he has refused to humble himself. He will not confess the Devil's power. He has blinded his heart." He looked about him and added, "I have some experience in these matters." The climbing sun was catching at the dew and there were tiny gold drops on the grass-blades and along the black thornbush stems. Sounds of scuttling and waking stirred in the earth, and a very small soft breeze just brushed the weeds. The Reverend Lapp reflected with satisfaction on his triumph in the matter of Thomas Clegg's salvation.

The Reverend Birdsong bowed his head and saved his breath.

From the waiting house, Micah saw them coming and shouted before he could remember to be quiet. Jabez woke, buzzing angrily like a wasp. Gramma peered at the arrivals and said, " 'Bout time. Who told you to come?"

"How is she? . ." said Birdsong.

"Dyin' likely," said Gramma bleakly. "That fat hump of a woman won't let me set foot inside. Dead and laid out by now, f'r all anybody tells me—No, she ain't!" she cried and clutched Jabez, who however was not at all disturbed by forebodings. Once he had found a banty hen quite dead inside Mr. Clegg's corncrib, but that was a hen and not Ma. He thought he was hungry and considered howling, but the reverends were more interesting than porridge and he held his tongue and set himself to stare.

"Mrs. Hasty's in with Ma, Reverend," Gideon said. "And Dorrie too."

"They flung me out," said Gramma, feeling she had not yet gotten the most out of the situation. "Six of Amos's young uns I fetched into this here vale of tears, and now they've flung me out. I wasn't much help to nobody, at that," she added.

The Reverend Lapp had his eye fixed on Gideon. "Your father should be here, where his duty lies," he said sternly.

He waited, but Gideon made him no answer.

Birdsong sat down on the step beside Gramma, and Sheby came and leaned against him. Micah said suddenly, "Gideon don't want to wander, Reverend Lapp. He don't want to no more than a dog wants to have fleas, but it has to be so because he was the first son of Pa and Pa was the first son of his pa and his pa—"

"Hush," said Gideon.

The Reverend Lapp drew himself up. "Let the wicked forsake his way," he exclaimed, "and the righteous man his thoughts. Wide is the gate and broad is the way that leadeth to destruction."

"Amen," said a voice from the meadow side.

They all turned like weathercocks to see who had spoken, and there was Mrs. Clegg, deep in black even at early dawn and looking for all the world like a jack-in-the-pulpit come out of the woods. She peered out from between black bonnet and black shawl and said to Gideon, "I heard your trouble and I've come to pray with you."

"Who told y' the news?" said Gramma, interested.

"Little Fox Jones," said Mrs. Clegg. "He's going about the village, telling how the young uns' ma has been struck down. I was real sorry to hear."

Micah said quickly, "She ain't struck down, she's birthing. There's to be a baby—"

"A girl one," said Sheby softly.

"Likely a boy," said Micah unthinking, and then he saw the tears spring into his sister's eyes. His heart smote him instantly, and he said, "A girl then, Sheby. It's no matter to me."

"A girl," said Sheby, cradling it in her arms. "A small un for me. She's to be named Jezebel out of the Holy Book."

The Reverend Lapp gave a cry of anguish. "Jezebel!"

There was the sound of running feet from inside the house, and the door flung open on Dorrie. She said, "Hush, be quiet," fiercely, and then she saw the Reverend Lapp with his mouth still open, and she said hastily, "I'm sorry, Reverend, but please don't be making a noise. The pains are on her bad again, and the baby's not yet come. It's like something's holding it back from coming—" She put her hand up against her mouth and then she took it away and said softly, "Please do be quiet," and went into the house.

Lapp said with absolute authority, "The Devil is holding the child back from coming. The Devil has placed his hand on this house and he will not let go. There is no true repentance here, and where pride and wilfulness and sin have been sowed, ye shall reap destruction." He turned and pointed a long finger at Gideon, and it trembled a little with the urgency that ran through him. "Gideon Briggs—"

"You leave that boy alone," said Gramma suddenly. "He ain't done you no harm and it ain't his fault he's called on to wander. He's no sinner, Gideon's not. He's as good a lad as ever got hisself borned, and I won't have you a-standin' and a japin' at him—"

Mrs. Clegg touched her arm timidly. "You must not argue with the reverend," she said. "He knows. You must remember that he knows. He saved my husband like a brand from the burning, and my husband died very holy."

"Pah!" said Gramma. "No holier'n a possum. Thomas Clegg lived ornery and he died ornery, mean as pizen water." She gave herself a flump, sitting there on the step, and looked around challengingly.

Mrs. Clegg stared at her. The Reverend Lapp said reprovingly, "Mr. Clegg died in the Lord."

"He did not," said Gramma. "He died narrer on his bed and as stubborn as our pig, no more holy than—" She stopped so short it might have been a summer lightning-stroke come on her with the hearing of her own words. Her jaw hung loose for a moment, and then she gave a fearsome wail and threw her skirt over her head, announcing from its muffling folds that she was a poor old woman and full of the misery.

For a space in time that lasted nearly forever, the Reverend Lapp stood turned to stone. Then he strode to Gramma, seized her by a bony shoulder and shook her out of her refuge. "Are you saying that Thomas Clegg never repented?" he demanded.

"He never saw the Angel of the Lord? You never prayed together?" His voice rose so he was near shouting.

Gramma sagged in his clutch and gave a loud snuffle, partly because his grip was so powerful and partly because she saw too late how she had undone herself.

"Answer me!" Lapp cried.

"Well, mebbe we didn't pray exactly," said Gramma. "Mebbe we didn't—" She searched out a bit of petticoat to sop her nose on. " 'Twarn't my fault, Reverend, he went so sudden. I was a-leanin' acrost his bed and arguin' that he should let Gideon have the cow, and him not sayin' one givin' word, and then—"

"The cow!" said Lapp. "He didn't even give you the cow?"

Gramma's second wail made a poor sickly shadow out of her first. Her skirt flew high and she vanished once more beneath it, howling mightily that she only wished it was her shroud.

Lapp turned from her, turned from them all. He put his hands across his eyes and stood like a lonely pillar, rigid and black.

"Oh dear, dear," said the Reverend Birdsong and gazed at Gramma and Mrs. Clegg in sincere distress, not quite certain which one was in greater need of spiritual consolation. He decided Mrs. Clegg was the more bereaved, and after a moment he said hesitantly, "My dear lady—"

She looked at him, mouselike, and burst into tears.

The Reverend Birdsong clucked.

Shadrach, great-eyed, said, "Was it never our cow at all?" Sheby put her head down on her knees. Jabez whimpered. Micah said "Sweet cow" in a voice of terrible longing and held fast to Gideon's hand.

"Eeee, dearies, I'm sorry," said Gramma from under her skirt. "I'm a miserable sinner."

"There, there," said Mr. Birdsong and patted both mourners.

Gramma remained in her hidey-hole, but Mrs. Clegg lifted her head, sighed terribly deep and wiped her eyes on her shawl. "Seems like I always knew it somehow, Reverend."

"Mrs. Clegg—"

"It never really seemed like Thomas to die in the Lord that way," she said, shaking her head. "He never really cared for the Lord, Thomas didn't."

Gramma popped out. "That's right," she said eagerly. "Never a kind word for the Lord did that man have, not even when the Reverend Lapp was trying to set him in a state of grace." She peeped at Lapp, but he just stood there like an old tree, his back to them and his hands hanging loose at his sides. After a moment, Gramma said hopefully, "Of course if he'd a-died in the Christian act of giving us the cow, that'd have been a great weight off his soul. Wouldn't it, Reverend, wouldn't it likely?" She reached out and jerked at Lapp's coattails.

From a great distance he returned to them. He looked down at her, then at all around him. As he stared and they stared back, he seemed to shrivel, growing meager and sad within his black coat and under his tall hat.

Finally, he turned to Birdsong and said dully, "I lost the battle for Thomas Clegg's soul."

"You cannot be certain of that," said Birdsong.

"The Devil was not subject to me," said Lapp bitterly.

Birdsong was silent. From within the house which had been so shut away from them, there came a cry, very sharp and bitten off like a hurt thing's. Gramma felt it cold in her bones and shivered all through. Mrs. Clegg made a fluttering move with her hands like a dove trying to quieten a nest. The children moved closer to Gideon.

"I think we ought to be praying," said the Reverend Birdsong, and went down on his knees in the grass.

One by one they kneeled like sheep in a pasture, until only the Reverend Lapp was left standing. He looked very dark in all the greenness about him, with the sun reaching to touch the clover, and the clouds, and the great trees with their roots deep in the land and their branches tangled in birds' nests and blue sky. He looked lost.

The Reverend Birdsong, his hands folded in prayer, gazed up at him, waiting. Lapp moved his own hands as if he had no idea where they should go or how serve him.

"Ain't nobody goin' to lead us in prayin'?" said Gramma loudly, finding the ground hard and herself bony. "You want I should lead us in prayin'?"

"Hush," said Birdsong.

"Everybody'll die while you're a-hushin' me," said Gramma crossly. "Not to mention my two legs breakin' off like sticks. I'll start us," she said, and did so at the top of her voice. "Oh, Lord, I'm a miserable sinner, I am."

The Reverend Lapp stirred as if the words had made him remember something, long forgotten. Then he looked around him slowly. And then, very suddenly, he gave a little bitter cry and bowed his head in his hands.

Once his head was bowed, it seemed that the way of prayer came easier to him. Very slow, slow as a leaf opening, he went down on his knees. They could almost hear the creaking of his rusty black clothes.

He put his hands up together, making a church of them, and he leaned his head so that it touched the tips of his prayerful fingers. "Dear Father," he said with awful difficulty, "dear Father, bless this house."

"Amen," said Birdsong.

The words were scarcely laid upon the air, fine as silk and with the little breeze blowing them about, when there came a new kind of cry from the house, a bleating and a wailing like a newborn lamb.

Sheby sprang to her feet and flew to the door, quick as a skimmer-fly. Jabez shouted, "It's a-comin', it's a-comin' " though not quite certain what he was announcing, and he beat Gramma happily over the head with his delighted hands. Gideon picked him up to hold under one arm and stood listening, waiting for the house to call again.

"Help me up, help me up," said Gramma, grabbing at Mrs. Clegg's trailing skirt and nearly pulling her down too. Birdsong bounced forward to recover them both, and at that moment Sheby came flinging out, her eyes like blue fires and her arms waving to push the crowding air out of her path. "Micah, Micah!" she cried. "Ma's birthed and you was wrong."

She got out of the doorway and there was Dorrie standing behind her, hands hanging tired at her sides but a soft look on her face. Over all the heads she sought out Gideon, and he came at her as if she had spoken his name.

" 'Tis a girl, Gideon," said Dorrie, "and all's well."

# CHAPTER TWENTY

ALL THE birds started to sing at once, calling from green branch to green branch, spreading the news of the sun and the birth of a baby, trill and chatter and call, ballad and canticle, scattered everywhere and very thriftless.

"I said 'twould be a girl," Gramma crowed. "Kickin' and fussin' the way it was, nigh drove its poor ma mad." She took a sudden notion to clasp Mrs. Clegg to her heart. "Pore thing, pore thing," said Gramma kindly. "No chick nor child of y'r own and me with seven right in my lap. You come along with me, dearie, and see the new young un. Its ma won't mind, she's real sociable."

Mrs. Clegg gave herself a sort of shake, but Gramma would not let her go and snatched her elbow. "Eh, let bygones be bygones, dearie. Some folks die in the Lord and some don't, y' can't hold a grudge agin 'em for it. I'm real sorry I got y'r hopes up, though."

Gideon picked Gramma gently off her clutch of Mrs. Clegg, like lifting a grasshopper loose from a hay tangle. "I'll bring the cow back to you tomorrow, Mrs. Clegg," he said. "And the calf too."

Mrs. Clegg looked at him sharply, and then all about her. She looked longest at the reverends, and finally at the house before she turned back to Gideon. "The cow was sick," she said, "and you took good care and brought the young calf safely. They're both yours for the keeping, Gideon. It wouldn't be Christian in me to say other."

Gramma gave a yelp. "Good cometh out of wickedness like it says in Scripture. Fountains sendin' out sweet water and bitter, both at the same time. I was a miserable sinner and a cow come out of my sins, fulfillin' the Good Book's word."

"A very liberal interpretation," said the Reverend Birdsong, "but to each according to his need. It is very Christian of you, Mrs. Clegg, it is indeed."

Gideon said in a voice that was full of gratefulness, "I want to thank you kindly. We'll be needing the milk special, with the baby and all, and it's a goodness in you."

Mrs. Clegg shook her head. "Maybe it will count on Mr. Clegg's side, come Judging Day. Maybe he repented him in the last moment." She turned to the Reverend Lapp and gazed at him hopefully with small bright eyes. "Could that be, Reverend, do you think that could be?"

He straightened slowly and sighed, looking down at the ground and up at the blue arc of June, at the house for which he had asked blessing, and finally at those about him. He said carefully, "Yes, I think it could be. It is not given for us to know very much, and we often act in error, but I think perhaps—" Once more he looked around him. "Gideon— Where is Gideon?"

Micah said, "He went all in a moment, Reverend. Likely gone to tell the cow. I'll go fetch him back." He would have leaped off without asking, but the Reverend Birdsong stretched out a staying hand.

"Leave him alone," he said. "Leave him alone, Micah."

Gideon could never have said why he left them at that moment, just when all was rejoicing, the baby birthed safely and the cow and the calf theirs again. He should have gone in to his ma perhaps, lying on the bed with the little round duckling head of Jezebel close to the crook of her arm. But Dorrie had told him all was well, Dorrie with her eyes shining as soft as gillyflowers, standing in the doorway and calling him to her side without words.

Dorrie would be glad about the cow and the calf, though it had been sinful of Gramma to invent a salvation, even if she was very old and feathered in her head. He thought about Gramma's wickedness for a moment, but what really mattered to him was knowing he could leave the cow and calf for Micah. It was no use troubling about the right and the wrong of it, and Mrs. Clegg seemed content enough.

The sun was up bright now, and Gideon stopped to look into the cow's shed as he went past. It was twilight-dark inside and pleasant and empty. Dust danced along a sun path that came through a chink, and the warm hay was all pressed down still where the calf had curled. A cat climbed out of it, shaking itself, saw Gideon and made a sound in its throat, then sat down to wash its ears.

Gideon went around to the lean-to where the pig, pleased with June, lay sideways, legs waving about to no purpose. He picked up a stick and leaned over to offer some scratching, and the pig grunted with pleasure. The ground around was rooted up with industry and greed, and kernels of corn made little golden patterns across its black richness.

Gideon tossed the stick away, and the pig snuffed in disappointment, then got up and trotted to the trough, nose buried in slops and tail curled as tight as a woodbine tendril.

Not knowing where he walked or why, Gideon turned toward the meadow, feeling a restlessness which was strange since all was settled and the baby come at last. He could not take his mind from Dorrie, looking so warm and alight just because a baby had been birthed, and he remembered how, when the calf was born, the sow had turned her gentle head and touched nose to the little thing. He wished suddenly that Dorrie was here with him now, going toward the meadow with her hand safe in his and her head at his shoulder. For a moment he felt such a terrible heartache that he stopped and stared around him with loss.

He would go, having no choice, and Dorrie would stay and wed someone else. They would be strangers when they met again, and the thought of that was cruel to him. But she would be safe with some good lad who would never go off and leave her with a baby coming. Like Pa had done.

He shook his head and stepped into the meadow where all June had come ahead of him, flowers running through the grass and an everlasting humming and buzzing wherever the brown bees clung, petals close and blue sky shut out while they scattered pollen and rocked in honey and bloom.

The cow saw him coming and lowed, and the calf who was growing fast came galloping to nuzzle his fingers, hard head pushing in rapture. Cow and calf belonged to them twice-over now, given and lost and given again.

He turned toward the meadow edge, and the calf ran after him for a bit until it was stung by a May-fly and twisted furiously to nip its own flank. The May-fly skittered away, riding the air, and the calf went back to its mother at a trot.

The trees at the meadow's edge were dark-leafed with summer, and under them ran a tangle of greenbrier and thicket and blackberry vines. A wild apple tree struggled to spread its branches, and Gideon thought how he had meant to cut the trees about it and give it leave to reach as it chose, all blossom in April and golden fruit in harvest time.

Perhaps Micah could cut the trees back when he was grown only a little more, taller and stronger and able to swing the axe easy so that it fell biting into green wood.

The apple tree was shivering-full of birds, busy with their nestlings, too busy to sing almost, quivering the twigs and making the pale leaves shake. Gideon whistled and, from deep in the tree's heart, something whistled back to him, very sweet, likely a wood-soul so near to Midsummer Eve.

He turned a blackberry bush out of his path and walked slowly through the woods that smelled fresh with the night damp still on them under leaves so close together. He could see the sky only in glimpses, summer blue so deep it might be drowned in like the Meander. It would never be so blue in China or Indy, if indeed they had sky there at all or only clouds and a great wind blowing.

He came to the clearing, where it lay in the woods like a cup of green, full of blossom and sunlight, thick moss on the twisting tree roots and a honeysuckle bush flowering yellow as pale as a dandelion's ghost.

As he stood looking about, Dorrie came so plain to him that, for a moment, he thought she was really there, and he said "Dorrie, love" out loud to the woods. Again he felt his heart very heavy in his breast, and he went slowly to the place where the earth lay a little rounded, the sleeping place of his mother and the baby that had scarcely lived.

He thought how his father had left them both and come back to find them gone, and such a terrible fierceness and anger burned up inside Gideon as was almost not to be borne. He said aloud to the clearing, all alone in it, "Maybe the Reverend spoke the truth. Maybe it is the Devil's curse against all of us."

But, even as he said the black words, he remembered how the Reverend Lapp had kneeled and asked a blessing on the house, and how on the very "Amen" the baby had been birthed. He would not believe that the Devil could speak against any of them: Dorrie, so quick to care; Micah who had gone alone to the deep woods at midnight; Ma, with all her waiting and all her babies; Gramma even, with her lies that were meant to be good.

In spite of all, the Devil had never found a dwelling place in the house Amos Briggs had left behind him. There was too much love about.

"There's a call," Gideon said to himself, standing there in summer's green world, "but there's no curse."

He was aware then, suddenly, of a great silence. The birds were still, the leaves hung quiet on the branches, there was no humming in the grass, no breeze through the flower petals. Gideon stood without moving and felt his heartbeat quicken.

Out of the stillness, came the call.

It was very low and whispered, but if it had been as loud as rolling thunder it could have come no plainer. It was a voice and a cry and it said his name and called him without words. There was no holding back against it. Hoeing man laid down his hoe, digging man laid down his spade, reaping man laid down his scythe. Gideon, with nothing to put aside, turned his face toward the summoning and walked blindly, scarce heeding where he set his feet.

The call cried him out of the clearing and back through the woods, and he had no thought for the reaching brambles or the lost path or the tree trunks that would have barred his way. Nothing breathed about him, and even his footfall was soundless.

He came so to the edge of the meadow he had left, and he pushed his way through the tall grass, following the call, through the motionless flowers, the silence where the brown bees had hummed. A white butterfly clung to a blossom, but its wings were as still as a winter's frost.

He saw the house in the distance and he yearned toward it so terribly that his heart almost left his breast, but there was no turning back now and no goodbye.

The call was rising and he could almost hear his name— "Gideon, Gideon."

He came to the heart of the meadow, and it was as if he stood in a bell-tower of sound so that the whole green stretch of it was shaken and the sky echoed. He stood still, not holding back but waiting to be told which way to turn to start on the journey that would leave all behind.

And, all at once, it was as if everything found voice, though nothing moved. The trees at the meadow's edge cried out, and the birds waked from their trance of stillness; the bushes, and the brown bees, and the flowered grass, the small animals in the woods, and the clouds in the sky. They spoke his name, he could hear it clearly, and the call poured itself into them and they into the call like brook into river.

Gideon stood silent and in wonder. It's like the land's talking to me, he thought.

Over and above and around the call, he could hear every sound he had ever heard—hoot of an owl in a gray dawn, split and crackle of lightning at a gashed dead tree, murmur of the Meander coming down from marshland, the cow lowing at milking time, the shush of the scythe and sigh of grass falling, brown earth gulping rain after dry times. He could hear the wind high in the tree branches, the ring of an axe and the wooden chunk of a log tossed on a pile, pig's grunt and cat's mew and hissing of geese, birds in full song and branches scraping each against each, skimmer-flies and bumblebees and grasshoppers in sunshine, and the clod and fall of earth turning under the plough.

As he listened, they all came together in one dominating call, one voice, and there was no mistaking it. It was the call to Gideon, first son of a first son, the call he must heed. But it did not cry to him from alien worlds of temple bells and white-tossed seas, of great ships, vast prairies and lonely rivers.

It cried to him from his own land.

Gideon stood straight, and such a happiness went through him that he could almost not breathe. "I'm to stay," he whispered. "My call's come at last, and it's cried me home."

He said the words, and in that moment the meadow was itself again. The wind took the grass tops, the butterfly opened its wings, and a grasshopper leaped at the sky.

Gideon turned and looked toward the house, seeing it for joy as if the sun shone at every window, bright on the threshold that would always know his step, bright on the roof that would shelter him and on the windows that looked out over land he need never leave.

As he watched, Dorrie came out of the house, her hair loose about her face and the gray of her dress like a wood dove. Micah ran to her, and Sheby, and she bent to them both but she was looking for someone else.

Gideon gazed at her for a moment with his whole heart, and then he lifted up his voice in a glad shout. "Dorrie!" he called. "Dorrie, I'm to stay!"

She heard him and for a moment she just stood staring. Then she gave a cry and ran to him, quick and light across the meadow, the clover bloom and the daisies catching at her skirt, and the sun and the soft wind catching at her hair.

He held out his arms, and in an instant she was in them and they had both come home.

*CHAPTER TWENTY-ONE*

MIDSUMMER MORNING dawned over grass heavy with dew, and the great woods turned quiet as the things of the short night fled the crowing of the cock, pulling their shadows close about them.

The sun was high in blue air by the time the Reverend Lapp sat down in his parlor to shape a sermon for Sunday. The room was even darker than usual because Mrs. Lapp mistrusted any day so long and bright as this one, but the Reverend was too absorbed to care, pursuing a verse which he believed to be from *Isaiah*.

When the knock came at his door, he rose, put the Bible under his arm and glanced down at the front of his black coat. All the buttons were fastened with great neatness, and he nodded tranquilly and went to answer the summons.

He was pleased to find the Reverend Birdsong on his doorstep. Birdsong was as full of scriptural sources as a hedgehog of prickles. Lapp said, "Ah, Birdsong! Do you by any chance recollect—" and stopped short.

In the Reverend Birdsong's left hand was his wicker case; in his right, his umbrella. This time, he bore no flowers.

"Birdsong?" said Lapp uncertainly.

"I have come to say goodbye," said Birdsong. "I woke this morning, and it came to me that this was the right day for setting out. Last year's cats are all having this year's kittens, and it is quite possible to overstay a welcome."

"But, my dear Birdsong!" said Lapp, distressed. "This is such a sudden decision, I hardly know— Surely you would not leave before the wedding?"

"I thought of that," Birdsong said soberly, "but I've heard the banns cried, which I dearly wanted. And we both know there should be only one minister to hear their vows."

"But you came here," Lapp said.

"I know." Birdsong nodded and looked down thoughtfully at the Bible in Lapp's hand, "There is a time to plant, you remember, and a time to pluck up that which is planted. I shall feel quite lonely for Greenwillow, I expect," he added cheerfully.

Lapp looked down at his boots.

"Well, now," said Birdsong, "I have said all I came to say." He opened his umbrella and held it over his head, and a hawthorn petal, long faded, fell out and fluttered to the ground. "This should keep the sun off my head very nicely. Dear, dear, I wish I had something to leave with you."

Lapp looked up at him.

"I must go," said Birdsong, nodding his head as if satisfied with everything about him, and turned on his heel. He went two steps down the path with the umbrella bobbing in the downpour of sun, and then he stopped and turned back. "I have the most curious feeling," said the Reverend Birdsong.

"Because you're leaving?" said Lapp.

"No, it's not that." He peered out, puzzled, from beneath the umbrella. "It is very odd. I feel as if, when I turn my back on the village, it will be gone."

"I've felt that too," said Lapp, nodding. "But it stays."

"Ah. In that case, I can go with a contented heart." He held out his hand, found he had the umbrella in it and took it back. "Goodbye, then," he said, and smiled.

"God be with you," said the Reverend Lapp, very gently.

## *The End*

# ABOUT THE AUTHOR

**B.J. Chute** (1913-1987). Born in rural Minnesota, Beatrice Joy Chute grew up the youngest of three sisters, all of whom rose to prominence in the literary world. A prolific writer, Chute authored numerous short stories that appeared in *Boy's Life*, *Woman's Day*, and *Ladies Home Journal*, as well as many novels, including *The Fields are White*, *The End of Loving*, *Katie: An Impertinent Fairy Tale* and *The Moon and the Thorn*. Chute was President of the American Center of P.E.N. from 1959-1961 and was instrumental in establishing P.E.N.'s writers fund. She also taught creative writing at Barnard College in New York City where she resided for much of her adult life. *Greenwillow*, one of her most beloved books, opened as a Broadway musical in 1960.